Life Extraordinaire

AN AUTOBIOGRAPHY

HEM RAJ VERMA

PRABHAT PRAKASHAN

Published by
PRABHAT PRAKASHAN PVT. LTD.
4/19 Asaf Ali Road,
New Delhi-110 002 (INDIA)
e-mail: prabhatbooks@gmail.com

ISBN 978-93-5562-731-5
LIFE EXTRAORDINAIRE: AN AUTOBIOGRAPHY
by Hem Raj Verma

Edition
First, 2026

Price
₹ 350 (Rupees Three Hundred Fifty Only)

Printed at
R-Tech Offset Printers, Delhi

To

My mother Narati Devi

whose boundless kindness and quiet wisdom shaped not just the course of my life, but the very essence of who I am. Her strength, compassion, and unwavering support continue to inspire me every day. This book is a tribute to her love, which has guided me through every step of my journey.

Foreword

My Father, My Icon

From as far back as I can remember, my father has been my guiding light, shaping my life with his remarkable persona. His influence on my journey, both personally and professionally, is immeasurable. A man who lives by the profound principles of the Bhagavad Gita, his wisdom, compassion, and strength are the pillars upon which I've built my own life.

His adherence to the art of living, rooted in the teachings of the Gita, is more than just a philosophy—it is a way of being. He approaches life's challenges with extraordinary grace and resilience, handling each moment, no matter how difficult, with a calmness that never ceases to amaze me. As a young girl, I was captivated by his ability to remain steadfast through life's trials. His visits to my school were always the highlight of my day. I would proudly announce, "My father is here, this is my daddy," basking in the pride of his intelligence and handsome demeanor, eager to share that joy with my friends and teachers.

Beyond his wisdom and strength, my father's compassion is what steered my professional aspirations. His kindness towards others and his commitment to making a positive impact on those around him became the foundation of my desire to help others. His presence is a constant source of inspiration. In many ways, my father's strength has become my own, guiding me in both my career and life.

I would be remiss not to take a moment in my father's autobiography to reflect on the influence of my mother, a woman with a heart of gold. Her kindness and compassion knew no bounds, and she had a unique ability to make everyone around her feel valued and loved. She taught me one of the most profound lessons of my life—to never hurt anyone, as this is the truest form of worship to God. Her gentle nature and wisdom shaped the way I see the world, reminding me to always approach life with kindness and compassion.

Together, my parents have been the cornerstone of my life. My father, with his wisdom and strength, and my mother, with her boundless compassion, have given me the foundation to become who I am today. Their lessons and love continue to inspire and guide me, reminding me of the incredible legacy they have built—one that I am honored to carry forward.

– Anjana

Love you Daddy!

❑

Author's Note

In the small vibrant village of Manvi, Punjab, my journey began. I was born in the year 1931, my childhood was filled with simple joys—playing with friends, learning from my parents and experiencing the rich culture of our village. These early years, during India's struggle for independence, instilled in me a sense of purpose and resilience.

Education became my guiding light, leading me from Manvi to Delhi College of Engineering (DCE). My days at DCE were a blend of rigorous studies and forming lifelong friendships. It was here that I discovered my passion for engineering and innovative thinking.

A pivotal point in my life was my marriage to Vidya while I was still a student. Vidya's unwavering support and love became my pillar of strength. Together, we balanced the demands of education and family life with determination.

With an engineering degree in hand, I pursued higher studies abroad. The international experience broadened my perspective and equipped me with valuable skills. It equipped me to envisage taking up roles of higher commitment, once I returned to India. I got an opportunity to work with various departments in state and central government of India, where my ideas contributed to the nation's development.

Rising from a small village to a high position in the Planning Commission was a testament to the transformative power of education and hard work. One true incident that stands out is the time I proposed a focal project that brought electricity to countless villages, including my own - Manvi, enriching lives of countless people.

This autobiography is a collection of my life's experiences and lessons. It captures the essence of a journey marked by challenges, perseverance, innovation and the enduring support of my family. I hope my story inspires future generations to dream big, work hard and achieve greater heights.

As you read these pages, may you find in my anecdotes of courage and determination a source of motivation to pursue your own dreams with passion and dedication.

❑

Contents

Chapter 1

The Humble Beginnings

Have you ever seen a beautiful sunset? I have; when I was a little boy, standing near the Shiv Mandir (Shivalya) in Manvi, the place where I grew up. As the sun sets, the sky turns vivid red and golden. The sky reflects this beautiful play of colours, and as you keep watching, the sun dips further till it seems to disappear into the sky. This is one of my favourite memories of my boyhood of standing by the Shiv Mandir, watching the sun go down and then racing home to my mother.

A journey that started on 21st April 1931 in Manvi, Punjab, has continued for over 93 years. Wandering across the globe, touching lives and pursuing careers gave me enriching experiences and unforgettable spiritual encounters. The journey has been nothing less than a blessing of Parampita Parmatma.

During the turbulent days of pre-independence and pre-partition India, my journey began in a small, vibrant village called Manvi, nestled in the heart of Punjab of erstwhile Patiala state in British Raj. There were only two small towns nearby - Amargarh and Malerkotla. My village was attached to Amargarh, being post office and police station. Malerkotla was capital of an independent state of Nawab.

I was born surrounded by the rich culture and hard-working spirit of the people in this land. Manvi wasn't just a village; it was the centre of a network of ten other villages—Jagowal, Doulowal, Dugri Roorki (Khurd), Roorki (Kalan), Chandurain, Boolapur, Senpura, Badla and more. These villages, with their intertwined lives and shared histories, formed a close-knit community under the canopy of Patiala state where tradition and heritage were deeply woven into the fabric of daily life.

Manvi stood out among the surrounding villages, not just because of its size but because it boasted a primary school, a beacon of learning, situated near our home. This school was more than a building; it was a symbol of hope and progress for the families in our village and the neighbouring ones. Education was seen as a way to elevate one's status and improve the quality of life, and having a primary school within such close proximity was a great privilege.

The nearest township, Amargarh, with its bustling market, post office and police station, was the hub where people from all the neighbouring villages converged for their daily needs. Amargarh was a cultural melting pot where people exchanged not only goods but also ideas, traditions and stories.

Another significant town was Malerkotla, the capital of the Nawab state, about 12 km away. Malerkotla was known for its high school, college and institutions that provided education up to the graduation level. This town promised opportunities for growth and development, attracting young minds eager to learn and carve out there profession.

Further still, Khanna Mandi in the Ludhiana district, located along the GT road, offered another high school. Khanna Mandi, situated on the bustling route between Ludhiana and Ambala, was a place where one could witness the confluence of rural and urban influences, a testament to the ever-evolving landscape of Punjab.

I grew up in a large joint family, a microcosm of values and traditions. My grandfather, Shri Rala Ram ji, was an illustrious Thumri musician, filling the air with melodies from a bygone era. His music was not just a profession but a way of life, a medium through which he expressed his emotions, thoughts and experiences. The soulful strains of his Thumri compositions often resonated through our home, creating an atmosphere of warmth and nostalgia.

My father, Shri Karam Chand ji, was the eldest son, known for his keen business acumen and his deep understanding of human relationships. He was a respected merchant of gold and silver and a pillar of our community. His wisdom and foresightedness guided many of his business decisions, and his ability to connect with people on a personal level earned him the respect and admiration of all who knew him.

Shri Karam Chand ji

He had a younger brother, Hansraj, and three sisters—Asha Devi, Poona Devi and Kala Devi. Our family was deeply rooted in the traditions and customs of our ancestors and each member played a significant role in upholding these values.

The joint family system provided a strong support network, where responsibilities were shared and decisions were made collectively. This sense of unity and togetherness was a cornerstone of our family life, shaping our interactions and relationships. There were so many of us living in that house, some of you may know what it is like to live with brothers and sisters and aunts and uncles and grandparents. We too lived like that-always surrounded by elders and children, old and young. We had so much fun-playing games, studying and going to school together. My mother, Narati Devi, was a wonderful cook. I may be old now, but I still remember the taste of kheer (a dish of rice and milk) she made for us that we ate sitting on the kitchen floor.

My father would wake up very early and go for long morning walks. He used to take care of his health and had meals at fixed regular timings. That may be the reason of his healthy and graceful life. I inculcated this habit from my father. I loved to accompany him but could go only some days when I didn't have school or classes to attend. We would set out from our home before the sun was up and light was only beginning to appear in the sky. It was usually cool and there would be pleasant breeze. I would hold his hand and walk quietly by his side for he would be saying his prayers under his breath. Then, something interesting would catch my attention and I would forget to be quiet.

My father would listen to all this chatter patiently with a smile on his face. We would walk to the end of the road, pass the ancient Kali Mata Mandir and then would take route to our farms. There, I would sit by his side and would listen to him talking to the caretakers about soil, manure and rains. I loved standing under those tall trees and looking into the swaying fronds. The light would flicker in and out between the leaves, teasing my eyes. I would close one eye and the light would seem even brighter, as the morning sun was winking back at me, telling me to have fun through the day.

I would hurry on ahead as we near our home, eager to tell my mother and elder sisters all about the things that I had seen. They, too, would listen to my stories as I prepared for the day. Other than my parents, we were many brothers and sisters in the house. My sister Devki used to take special care of me. I think she was especially fond of me as I was not as naughty as other children. My Bhabhi Kaushalya, wife of elder brother Dev Raj would get up early morning and prepare breakfast for me and prepare me for going to school. I was quite dreamy and loved to spend time on my own, either on my house rooftop watching the birds fly around or looking at the patterns of clouds.

My mind was always full of questions, like - why can birds fly but not me? Does the sun fall at the end of the day? I asked these questions to elders. I always looked at Dhruv Tara, the brightest star in the sky. My father was the first person to inspire me to study, to reach for the sky and shine like the brightest star.

At that time there were very few books available for children to read. I was always lost in the pages of the magazine Guncha, sent by the government of Patiala to school for children to read. I remember during World War - 2, there was a severe shortage of everyday items. Things were available only in small quantities. My father would say, see Hem, you must study hard and go to big school. You should go out there and see more of this world.

The days of my earliest childhood were filled with many moments of happiness and some sad days. I kept the faith in my parents and brothers and teachers and looked forward to days of hard work and learning. I realise now that it was a happy and a time filled with contentment.

The family faced a significant tragedy when my mother passed away at the age of 40. At that time, I was just 16 years old. Her memory, though faint, remains tenderly etched in my heart. Her untimely demise left a void in our lives, but it also brought our family closer together, reinforcing the bonds of love and support that held us together. My eldest brother, Dev Raj, took on the role of a guiding star, inspiring and supporting me throughout my educational journey. Without his steadfast support, my life might have taken a very different path. My two elder brothers, Devraj and Desraj expired at the age about 60 & 65 years respectively.

My father Shri Karam Chand Ji, was very competent, both in profession and business. He maintained cordial relations with all those he met, that is, relatives, clients and people in the village. He had been helpful all the time in life to whoever approached him for help financial aid or otherwise. In social life, also, he was liberal in helping people. He lived a dignified and blemish less life up to the age of 90 years.

During my childhood, I remember the day when I was first admitted in the primary school. My father took me to the school headmaster and requested him to admit me in the school. In those days in villages, there were no sweet shops; usually at the time of admission in the school, parents used to distribute Gud, Jaggery or Shakkar. He brought Gud, Shakkar and distributed in the school. At that time, I was about five years old. I do not remember much about my childhood before I went to school for the first time. The school was a one big hall and separate room for office records. The big hall was divided in four areas; one for each class. In front of this building, there was open area which was maintained by the school. During winter and summer, this area was also being used by students.

I was the monitor of the class and was always selected as the monitor unanimously without any competition. The teachers chose me and found me suitable to head the class. I was responsible to discipline my class, to keep the classroom clean and get the water sprayed in the open area of the school so that the classes can be conducted there. I even had to open and lock the school.

We used to write on Takti with a wooden Kalam. There was no paper. We had to clean our Takti with Kacchi Mitti and dry it under the sun. We used to sharpen our Kalam as we were not allowed to use the pen in the school. That era was very different, we didn't have electricity in those days. In the absence of electricity, we used to study in small mustard oil lamps. The lamps were costly, four students invariably used to share and study in one lamp to save the cost. After sometime, when import of kerosene oil started, we shifted to kerosene oil lamps. These lamps, though humble, cast a warm glow that became a symbol of our earnest quest for knowledge.

The seasons in Manvi were extreme and often unforgiving. During the peak summer, the hot winds, known as loo, would blow fiercely, making the air feel like a furnace. We often had to drape wet cloths over our faces to stay cool. Conversely, the winters brought chilling winds that swept through the village, covering the ground with a frost-like layer. Sometimes, the top

layer of water in ponds would freeze into a thin sheet of ice. To escape the blistering heat in summers, our teachers often held classes in a nearby mango grove. The cool shade of the mango trees provided a much-needed respite from the relentless sun, turning our lessons into a more pleasant experience. The school had wooden benches which were being used for senior classes like third and fourth and junior class students usually sat on mats spread on the ground. There was no clock in the school. Time for starting at the school was usually decided on the location of the sun at a particular point. Time was calculated from the position of the sun. During last two months of the season, the teacher used to organise tuition classes. Teacher used to charge Re.1 for first class Rs. 2 for second class, Rs.3 third class and so on. During evening, children of my age, both girls and boys, used to get together and play. There were not many opportunities for children to play. At times, we used to play luka chhupi, gilli danda, akharot, ritha, banta etc. We would play kabaddi, if the group size allowed.

My father was one of the most respected man in the village. Any person in the village having any financial and social problem used to approach him for help and he always helped them. I think I should mention an interesting episode here. He used to take me around some village on weekends; mostly on Sundays for collection of loan money. Village people used to wait for me to come and read the letters which they had received during the week. At every house, they used to offer me milk with lots of cream (Malai). It was impossible for me to consume the quantity of the milk with Malai offered to me at every house, for this reason I would, sometimes avoid going with him.

I also used to help my father in a shop and in this process I learnt to make some items of jewellery independently. The experience helped me in enhancing clarity of concepts when I joined Mechanical Engineering at Delhi College of Engineering.

After passing fourth class from the village school, I joined a middle school at village Chounda. Most of my education in primary school was in Urdu language. In the fifth class, we were offered English and Persian (Pharsi) for the first time. I liked Persian language and found it very interesting. I studied Persian for four years in the middle school.

Hem Raj Verma, Dev Raj Verma and Des Raj Verma

Devraj was the eldest among my brothers; he worked with my father. My father handed over all responsibility of running family business to him and retired. Though, he continued helping my brother in family matters and business. Devraj was very intelligent and proficient in running the family business. He also almost took over as a head of the family after the retirement of my father from the family business after the death of my mother. Devraj took over the responsibility of organising marriages of younger brothers and sisters. He was a very emotional and religious person. He always helped family members in business and other family matters.

Devraj was not just a brother; he was a mentor, a friend and a source of strength to us. His unwavering belief in my potential fuelled my pursuit of an engineering education in Delhi, a journey that would shape my future significantly. He encouraged me to dream big and provided the resources and guidance I needed to achieve my goals. He also motivated and supported me in pursuing engineering in Delhi. Without his support, I would not have taken up my education in engineering. What I am today is because of his motivation, guidance and support. His support was instrumental in helping me navigate the challenges and obstacles I encountered along the way.

He was a beacon of intelligence and dedication. He diligently assisted our father in the family business from a young age, gradually becoming the family's leader. When our father retired, Devraj seamlessly took over the reins, managing both business and family responsibilities. His vision in fact upgraded the status of our family in the society. He arranged the marriages of our younger siblings and helped them settle into their new lives.

My Bhabhi was very devoted to the family. She was always busy in household chores and never interfered in any business or family matters. I would like to mention that my Bhabhi gave birth to three children but all of them could not survive for more than 3-4 days. Thereafter, as suggested by our well-wishers in the village, my father organised Bhagwad Saptah in our home. Pandits from Mansa town near Patiala were invited and they performed 'Bhagwad' in our house. My bhabhi and brother were later blessed with 5 children and all of them survived.

Desraj, the middle brother, also played a crucial role in our family dynamics. From his early childhood, Desraj spent most of his time in Malerkotla with our father's maternal uncle, who had no children of his own. This arrangement, suggested by our grandmother, was intended to provide companionship and support to her brother. Desraj received his education in Malerkotla and eventually secured a job with the Government of India in Delhi, working in the Ministry of Agriculture. His journey, marked by dedication and perseverance, added another layer to the rich tapestry of our family history.

The practice of using jewellery as collateral was more than a financial transaction; it symbolised the community's values and mutual trust. Families would provide a small advance, while the remaining amount was converted into a loan repayable over time based on agricultural yields. This approach of my father showcased not only them being financial savvy but also their commitment to community support. My father exemplified this spirit, a master of relationships that stretched beyond business. My father's outreach extended beyond transactions, embracing every interaction, be it with kin, clients or fellow villagers. His heart and hand were open to all who sought his assistance, be it of initial or more nature, his generosity knew no bounds, he was a benefactor of community endeavours, patron festivals and art forms that grace the village. Whether it was the Ram Leela or the troops that painted the village with festive colours, he was everyone's favourite and was synonymously chosen by everyone. He lived in the heart of people.

As a young Hemraj, I watched my father's life tapestry of these values, generosity and humility with itself into his own narrative. He left an indelible mark, a testament to a life lived with dignity and purpose. His legacy, shimmered with integrity and resonated with future generations. These values subtly shaped my own personality, becoming an integral part of who I am.

My mother died at a very young age, i.e., at 40 at that time. I was not even in my teens when I saw her passed away. I have got very soft and loving memories of her. She was there to listen to me and used to do a lot of household work. She was very hard-working as whenever I used to come from school, she used to be busy with some work or other. In those days, life of women was not easy. Since, cow dung is considered to be very auspicious in the houses, so it was a ritual of cleaning the house with the use of cow dung. The ladies would collect cow dung in a big bucket. This was done by my mother in our house. She used to mix cow dung with water and apply on the floor/walls of the house. This was a prominent ritual and took a lot of efforts. On some occasions, my mother used to prepare kheer of rice, milk and sugarcane juice. It took a lot of efforts. Since there was no Gas at that time, she used to make it on Mitti ka Chulha and wood. Because of the Chulha, its colour used to be pinkish. I still remember its taste, it was very rare and we cannot find it in today's time. My mother was born in a village called Isra near Amargarh and she had no brother. She also used to call my eldest brother, Devraj, as 'bhai' (brother).

My father lived a life marked by generosity and compassion. He was a pillar of our community, always ready to help anyone in need, whether financially or otherwise. His contributions to social causes were often anonymous, reflecting his humility and desire to serve without seeking recognition.

He instilled in us the values of hard work, integrity and empathy. His life was a testament to the power of kindness and the impact a person can have on their community. Even after his retirement, he continued to support our family and the village, ensuring that his legacy of generosity and compassion lived on.

Desraj, too, made significant contributions to our family and community. His work with the Government of India allowed him to support his family and contribute to the development of our nation. Despite the challenges he faced, Desraj remained committed to his responsibilities, ensuring that his children received a good education and got well-settled in life. He was fond of playing chess and his friend Nand Lal from Jallunder always joined him. Incidentally, Nandlal from a Jain family was married to a girl from Malerkotla. Nandlal was a good football player and was a great inspiration to my brother Desraj. My brother Desraj used to come to our home at Manvi from Malerkotla during vacations. He was fond of kite flying. We used to make our own kites at home.

Inspired by my family's legacy of resilience, dedication and community spirit, I embarked on my own journey. My engineering education in Delhi opened up new horizons, allowing me to achieve remarkable milestones. The values instilled in me by my family guided me throughout my life, shaping me into the person I am today.

Manvi, like many other villages in Punjab, was a melting pot of various cultures, traditions and professions. Our village was home to a diverse mix of jats, sikhs, brahmins, khatris, banias, blacksmiths, carpenters and tailors. This diversity added a rich texture to our daily lives, with each community contributing its unique skills, traditions and customs to the collective tapestry of village life.

One of the most cherished memories of my childhood is the sound of my grandfather's Thumri music. Shri Rala Ramji was a master of this classical music form and his performances were a source of pride and joy of our villagers during the festivals and Melas in the adjoining villages.

Thumri, with its emotive and expressive style, was not just music; it was a narrative of emotions, a reflection of the human soul.

Agriculture was the backbone of our village economy. The vast fields surrounding Manvi were filled with crops of wheat, maize and various vegetables. The agricultural cycle dictated the rhythm of our lives, with sowing, harvesting and threshing, marking the key phases of the year. The monsoon rains were eagerly awaited, as they determined the success of the harvest. Festivals like Baisakhi, which celebrated the harvest, were major events filled with joy, music and dance. My father always awaited the harvest as he used to get his loan money back after the Agriculture yield.

Living in a joint family was an experience that shaped my understanding of relationships, responsibilities and community. Our household was a bustling hub of activity, with multiple generations living under one roof. This arrangement had its challenges, but it also provided a strong bond and support system. Decisions were made collectively and responsibilities were shared, ensuring that no one bears the burden alone.

Festivals and community celebrations were an integral part of our lives. Diwali, Holi and Baisakhi were celebrated with great enthusiasm, bringing together people from all walks of life. These festivals were not just about rituals; they were about community bonding, sharing and creating memories. The Ram Leela performances, musical troupes and other cultural events added vibrancy to our village life, making it a rich tapestry of traditions and joy.

Life Without Modern Conveniences

There was no tap water in the village. People used to bring few pitchers of water from the common well for use in the kitchen and for other daily chores. Male members usually used to bathe at the common well of the village or wells at the nearby Gurudwara or Shiv Mandir, which were outside the village. My family usually had one or two buffaloes for milk and ghee. There was no scarcity of milk or ghee to be used in the family. Vanaspati oil was not used by villagers, at that time. Some people used to buy it from the nearby town, hiding it from others in the village as it was considered a taboo. My father had one younger brother Hansraj and three sisters younger than him- Asha Devi, Poona Devi and Kala Devi. My father was very keen that, my uncle, should go for higher studies. He got him admitted him in a school at Khanna Mandi. Another person- Hari Singh from village and a friend of my uncle were also admitted in the high school there. He was son of Lambradar Sh. Sultan Baksh. Both friends passed matriculation and were highest educated people in our village at that time. In those days, a Lambradar in a village was considered to be repesentative of the state government, British Raj. He was assigned the duty of collection of taxes from the agriculture income from the villages.

My uncle, Hansraj's, journey in education did not stop at matriculation. He later became a teacher, working initially at Chaunda's middle school and then at Pyal's high school. His dedication to his profession and his commitment to imparting knowledge were commendable. He would pedal approximately 16 kilometers every day on his bicycle to reach Pyal, braving the extreme weather conditions of Punjab. The scorching heat of summer and the biting cold of winter did not deter him from fulfilling his duties as a teacher. His perseverance and resilience were qualities that I deeply admired and sought to emulate in my own life.

Our family business extended beyond trade to encompass the rituals and celebrations of life. We were deeply involved in the community, providing jewellery on credit to those who couldn't afford it outright, with the understanding that the balance would be paid over time from their agricultural yields. This practice exemplified our financial astuteness and community-oriented spirit. It was a unique system built on trust and mutual respect, reflecting the close-knit nature of our village society.

My father was not just a merchant but a community cornerstone. He adorned his business dealings with empathy and warmth, weaving relationships that extended beyond mere transactions. He was generous, a benefactor of community endeavours, and a patron of festivals and art forms that graced the village. His benevolence was often anonymous, a silent stream that left a lasting impact on those uplifted by his generosity. Despite his gentle soul, he was also a man of authority, serving as the village headman, or Sarpanch, for many years. His leadership was characterised by fairness, integrity, and a deep sense of responsibility towards the well-being of our village.

Understanding the economic landscape of that era provides context to our lives. In the years 1936-37, desi ghee was being sold at 4 rupees per kilogram. These prices reflected the simpler life of those times, where commodities were much cheaper compared to today's standards. The economic conditions shaped our daily lives and influenced our decisions and priorities.

The village economy was primarily agrarian, with most families relying on agriculture for their livelihood. Our family, however, had diversified into the jewellery business, which provided a stable and lucrative source of income. The ability to extend credit to villagers for jewellery purchases was a testament to our financial stability and the trust we had built within the community. This practice not only supported our business but also strengthened the bonds of trust and mutual dependence that held our village together.

The sense of community and belonging that I experienced growing up in Manvi has been a constant source of strength and inspiration. The bonds of trust, mutual respect, and shared values that characterised our village life have been the bedrock of my personal and professional relationships.

Education has played a pivotal role in my life, opening up new horizons and providing the tools needed to navigate the complexities of the modern world. The support and encouragement from my family, especially my brother Dev Raj, were instrumental in my educational journey, allowing me to achieve my goals and contribute meaningfully to society.

As I continue my journey, I am committed to upholding the values and principles that have guided me so far. The legacy of my family, the lessons learned, and the experiences gained will continue to light the way for future generations. My story is a testament to the power of resilience, dedication and community spirit.

The post-independence era brought about significant changes and opportunities. The establishment of new educational institutions, the development of infrastructure and the overall modernisation of society opened up new avenues for growth and progress.

My journey to Delhi for higher education was a transformative experience. The bustling city, with its diverse population and vibrant culture, was a stark contrast to the quiet, close-knit community of Manvi. Pursuing an engineering degree in Delhi broadened my horizons, exposing me to new ideas, technologies and ways of thinking. It was a time of personal growth and self-discovery, laying the foundation for my future career. I may add that the year 1952, I got admission in the college of Engineering in Delhi. In North India up to Bombay, there were only 3 Engineering Colleges, in Roorkee, Varanasi and Delhi.

My educational journey began in the humble surroundings of Manvi. After passing the fourth class board examination with the highest marks in Patiala state, I received a scholarship from the state government. I moved to a middle school in Chaunda for the fifth class. The school was about 6 kms from our village, and we travelled on foot, often enjoying playful activities along the way. During winters, the journey was challenging due to the cold, and in summer, we would jump into the canal to cool off.

World War II brought significant changes. There were food shortages, and students were asked to bring their share of wheat every month to Hostel as the school couldn't purchase it from the market. Our teachers organised evening tuition classes, charging a small fee. Despite the hardships, we remained committed to our studies.

In 1947, I joined the high school in Khanna, Ludhiana district. The school had a huge campus, and I stayed in the hostel, which provided a structured environment for studies and extracurricular activities like football. I passed matriculation with high marks and moved to DM College in Moga, where I studied science. My friend Harbhagwan Dunga was also in my class. The friendship that started in the school continued to be there throughout our lives. I believe friends are very important in your life. They can make you or they can break you. I cherish my moments shared with them.

In 1952, I was selected for the mechanical engineering course at Delhi Polytechnic, which later became affiliated with Delhi University. The transition from a national diploma to a degree program was a result of student agitation for recognised degrees. I graduated in 1958 with a BE in Mechanical Engineering, which paved the way for my professional career.

Studying in the USA was a transformative experience. I gained advanced knowledge in industrial engineering, which I was eager to apply back in India. The exposure to different cultures and advanced technologies broadened my horizons and deepened my understanding of engineering principle.

Upon returning to India, I was committed to sharing my newfound knowledge and experience. I worked on various projects that contributed to India's industrial growth. My efforts were focused on improving productivity and efficiency in manufacturing processes, aligning with the goals of the National Productivity Council.

The Role of Education

Education has played a pivotal role in my life, opening up new horizons and providing the tools needed to navigate the complexities of the modern world. The support and encouragement from my family, especially my brother Dev Raj, were instrumental in my educational journey, allowing me to achieve my goals and contribute meaningfully to society. The value of education is something I have strived to pass on to the next generation, ensuring that they too, have the opportunities to learn, grow and succeed.

After completing my education, I embarked on a career that allowed me to apply my knowledge and skills in practical ways. My professional journey was marked by challenges, successes, and continuous learning. The values of hard work, integrity, and community service instilled in me by my family guided me throughout my career, helping me navigate the complexities of the modern world.

Reflections on my Family

I was blessed with four daughters and one son: Geeta, Namita, Anjana, Alka and Somesh. Having a son after four daughters brought immense joy and a unique sense of fulfillment. Each of my children has enriched my life in countless ways.

My Family:

- **Geeta:** My eldest daughter born in 1954, left us early in 1968 after a brief illness.
- **Namita:** Born in 1961. Married to Adv. Joginder Pal Jindal, their children, Dr. Mohit Jindal and Er. Shefali Gupta, have made us proud. Dr. Mohit Jindal and his wife, Dr. Kirti Garg, are blessed with two wonderful grandchildren, Myra and Kyansh. Er. Shefali Gupta and her husband, Er. Chirag Gupta, have a son, Ishir.

- **Anjana:** Born in 1964. Married to Dr. Sharwan Gupta, their family is an epitome of dedication and success. Their children, Er. Preity Gupta (MBA) and Er. Divyansh Gupta (Post Graduate in Data Analytics, Ireland), are exemplary in their respective fields. Er. Preity Gupta, married to Er. Gaurav Garg, continues to inspire us.
- **Alka:** Born in 1967. Married to Er. C. D. Kaushal, their son Er. Gagan Kaushal is a bright star in our family. He is a Post- Graduate from USA and is now working in USA. Alka left for her heavenly abode in November 2014.
- **Somesh:** Born in 1970. My only son, is married to Simi Verma, has given us the joy of two more grandchildren, Ishita Verma (Post-Graduate in Corporate Finance, UK) and Dhruv Verma (Post-Graduate in International Management, UK). Somesh an Engineering and MBA graduate is running his own business in Medical Devices successfully.

Each member of my family brings their own light and love, making my journey truly blessed and fulfilling.

❑

Chapter 2

Childhood in Manvi

Our village lacked many modern conveniences. There was no tap water, so we fetched water from the common well for use in the kitchen and for use by ladies of the house. Male members usually bathe at the common well or at a smaller well near the Gurudwara or Shiv Mandir outside the village. Our family usually kept one or two buffaloes for milk and ghee, so we never faced shortages of these essentials. Using Vanaspati oil was taboo in those day, and those who did kept it a secret. Occasionally, I accompanied my father to the fields to gather green for our cattle, a task that made me feel helpful and responsible.

The Simple Joys of Village Life

Growing up in Manvi was a unique experience. Life was simple, yet rich with traditions and communal bonds. Our daily routines were punctuated with tasks that connected us to the land and to each other. Fetching water from the common well, helping with household chores and participating in seasonal activities were all part of our lives.

The Importance of Community

Our village was a close-knit community where everyone knew each other. The sense of belonging was strong and the support system was robust. Whenever there was a celebration or a crisis, the entire village would come together. This collective spirit was especially evident during festivals and communal events. The bonds formed were based on mutual respect and shared experiences.

Festivals and Celebrations

Festivals were a significant part of our lives. Diwali, Holi and Baisakhi were celebrated with great enthusiasm. Diwali, the festival of lights, transformed our village into a glittering wonderland. Homes were decorated with oil lamps and rangoli designs, and the air was filled with the sound of laughter and fireworks. Holi, the festival of colours, brought everyone together in a riot of hues. We would smear each other with vibrant colours and dance to the beat of drums. Baisakhi, marking the harvest season, was a time of joy and gratitude. The entire village would gather to celebrate with music, dance and feasts.

My Father's Influence

My father's influence on my life was profound. He was a man of principles, integrity and compassion. His actions spoke louder than words and I learned the value of kindness and generosity from him. He was always ready to help those in need, whether it was a financial matter or a personal issue. His guidance and support were instrumental in shaping my character and values.

Learning beyond the Classroom

Education in our village wasn't limited to the classroom. I learned many valuable lessons through everyday experiences. Helping my father in the shop, fetching water from the well and assisting with household chores taught me the importance of hard work and responsibility. These tasks also provided opportunities for bonding with family members and learning about our traditions and customs.

Childhood Fascination with Mantras

One of the most intriguing aspects of my childhood was the mantras I learned. These mystical chants had a profound impact on me. The first mantra allowed me to remove honeycombs without being stung by bees. I was amazed at how the bees remained calm and harmless as I carefully took the honey. The second mantra enabled me to pass a large needle through my thigh without feeling pain or drawing blood. This feat astonished my friends and me. Looking back, I am still in awe of how these mantras worked and the power they seemed to hold.

The Power of Mantras

Mantras are sacred sounds, words or phrases that are chanted to invoke spiritual energy and connect with the divine. In many spiritual traditions, mantras are believed to possess powerful vibrational energies that can influence the mind, body and environment.

1. **Spiritual Connection:** Mantras serve as a bridge between the material and spiritual realms. Chanting them with devotion and focus can help individuals attain higher states of consciousness and spiritual awakening.
2. **Mental Focus and Calm:** Mantras can induce a state of deep concentration and tranquility. The repetitive nature of chanting helps quiet the mind, reduce stress and enhance mental clarity.
3. **Healing and Protection:** Many believe that mantras have healing properties. They are used to protect against negative energies, promote physical and emotional healing, and bring about positive changes in one's life.

Reflections on My Early Years

As I reflect on my early years, I am filled with gratitude for the experiences and lessons that shaped me. Growing up in Manvi, with its simple yet rich way of life, instilled in me values that have guided me throughout my life. The sense of community, the importance of hard work and the value of kindness and generosity are principles that I carry with me to this day.

The Influence of Childhood Memories

Memories are powerful. They shape our identity, influence our decisions and guide our actions. The memories of my childhood in Manvi are a treasure trove of experiences that have enriched my life. They remind me of where I come from and the values that have shaped me. These memories are a testament to the enduring power of a simple, honest and meaningful life.

The Role of Early Childhood Values

The values that children absorb when they are tender become an integral part of their personality. During these formative years, the lessons learned and the examples set by parents and caregivers create a lasting impression. This early influence plays a crucial role in shaping a child's character and guiding their future actions.

The Enduring Power of Memories

The memories of my childhood in Manvi serve as a constant reminder of the values that have shaped me. They are a source of inspiration and strength, reminding me of the simple, honest and meaningful life that my parents exemplified. These memories are not just a recollection of the past but a guiding light for the future.

Reflecting on these experiences, I realise how deeply they have influenced my decisions and actions. The power of memories lies in their ability to connect us to our roots, reinforce our values and shape our identity. They remind us of who we are and what we stand for, ensuring that the lessons learned in our formative years continue to guide us throughout our lives.

The Journey Continues

The journey of life is filled with challenges and opportunities. The experiences of my early years in Manvi have prepared me for this journey. They have given me the strength and resilience to face whatever comes my way.

A Life of Purpose

A life of purpose is one that is guided by values and principles. The lessons I learned during my early years in Manvi have given me a sense of purpose. The journey of life is filled with challenges and opportunities. A life of purpose is one that is guided by values and principles. The lessons I learned during my early years in Manvi have given me a sense of purpose. They have guided my actions and decisions and shaped my character. It has taught me the importance of helping and supporting others. Hard work has always been a cornerstone of my life.

Why I Chose to Be an Engineer

Early Inspirations

In Manvi, I was surrounded by skilled craftsmen, including blacksmiths and carpenters, who made intricate bullock carts and other essential agriculture tools. I remember one particular mistri, a skilled artisan, who proudly claimed, "We are engineers, doing the work of engineers. Yet, engineers from the city come here as bosses." This statement left a deep impression on me. I realised that the work these craftsmendid was complex and essential, and they deserved respect and recognition for their skills.

The Canal Project

When I was in the 8th class, a significant canal and road project began near our village. The arrival of the engineers was a major event. People spoke of the "engineer sahib" with great respect. Seeing the respect and admiration that the engineers commanded, I thought to myself, "being an engineer is a good and respectable profession."

Also, the son of chairman of the my school management committee, an engineer, was given extra ordinary respect. This inspired me to consider engineering as a future career.

A Fortunate Encounter

My journey towards becoming an engineer took a decisive turn during my college years. One day, I learnt about a vacancy at Delhi College of Engineering. On enquiring, I was told that only the Principal can give details about the vacancies, but he had not been coming to college for the last few days. I decided to visit the principal's house to inquire about the vacancies. When I arrived, his daughter answered the door. I explained my purpose and she informed me that her father was not well. I felt awkward and quickly apologised for the intrusion. Her demeanour softened and she smiled, inviting me inside to meet her father.

She led me to her father who, despite his illness, listened to my request as it was last day to file my application in Engineering College at Delhi. This fortunate encounter enabled me to secure a place at the college and set me on the path to becoming an engineer.

Reflections on My Journey

Looking back, I realise how a series of small but significant experiences shaped my career choice. The respect for engineers in my village, the inspiration from skilled craftsmen and the kindness of the principal's daughter all played a role in my journey. Each experience reinforced my belief in the value of engineering and the respect it commanded.

Conclusion

The journey to becoming an engineer was filled with moments of inspiration and opportunities seized. It taught me that perseverance, respect for hard work and the kindness of others could open doors to new possibilities. These lessons from my early years in Manvi have stayed with me, guiding my actions and decisions and shaping my life's purpose.

Believing in hard work and destiny has shown me that, sometimes, the path to success is a combination of effort, luck and the opportunities that come our way. The seat I got in the engineering college was not just a matter of luck, but also a testament to the belief that God has a plan for each of us.

The Gift of Heritage

My heritage is a gift that I cherish deeply. It is a wellspring of pride and strength, a tapestry woven with the traditions, values and experiences of my early years. This precious inheritance has profoundly shaped my identity and continues to guide me as I navigate through life.

Strength and Resilience

The values I inherited from my heritage have provided me with the strength and resilience to face life's challenges. From a young age, I have learnt the importance of hard work, integrity and compassion. These values were not just taught but were live examples set by my parents and elders. The work ethic and perseverance of my father, the kindness and nurturing spirit of my mother and the communal harmony of our village community have all been integral in shaping my character and fortitude.

Guiding Principles

The lessons and values of my heritage serve as guiding principles in my life. They influence my decisions, actions and interactions with others. I had the opportunity of dealing with technical staff, highly placed bureaucrats, top level successful industrialists of the country and foreign dignitaries that influenced my work culture through dedication and decision taking capabilities.

Cultural Richness and A Lasting Legacy

As I journeyed through life, my heritage remains a lasting legacy that I strive to uphold and pass on to future generations. It is a living entity, evolving yet rooted in the timeless values and traditions of my past. By embracing my heritage, I honour the sacrifices and contributions of those who came before me, ensuring that their legacy endures.

Conclusion

In essence, my heritage is a precious gift that has shaped my identity and continues to guide me. It is a source of pride, strength, and inspiration, deeply embedded in the traditions, values, and experiences of my early years. As I continue my journey, I carry this heritage with me, confident that it will light my path and enrich my life in countless ways.

Introduction to My Spiritual Journey

As I grew older, I found myself increasingly drawn towards spirituality. My belief in God deepened, providing me with a profound sense of strength and solace. This inner calling sparked a desire to explore the world of meditation, marking the beginning of my spiritual journey. At the age of 7 to 11 years, I was regularly going to Shiv Mandir each morning and offered pooja before I started going to middle school to join 5th class at Chaunda.

A Deepening Belief in God

The cornerstone of my spiritual awakening was a deepening belief in God. This belief was not merely a passive faith but an active source of guidance and comfort. Turning to God in moments of need offered me clarity and inner peace, helping me navigate life's challenges with renewed confidence.

The Pursuit of Meditation

With my growing spiritual inclination, I developed a strong desire to learn meditation. The practice of meditation, with its promise of inner tranquility and divine connection, captivated me. I was eager to explore this ancient discipline, hoping to cultivate a deeper sense of self-awareness and spiritual growth.

In the year 1969, I learnt the art of Meditation, in Chandigarh from disciples of Mahesh Yogi, who had devised a technique for development of improving memory and transcendental intelligence. I continue to practice that technique which I adopted in my life.

The Start of a Transformative Journey

My journey into spirituality began with a determined effort to understand and practice meditation. I sought out teachers and resources to guide me, dedicating myself to developing a meaningful and disciplined meditation routine. This journey was about more than just finding peace; it was about discovering my place in the universe and fostering a closer relationship with the divine.

The Impact of Spirituality

Embracing spirituality brought about profound changes in my life. Meditation became a daily practice that grounded me, providing a sense of calm and balance amidst the chaos of everyday life. It taught me to live in the present moment, appreciate life's beauty and remain resilient in the face of adversity.

A Lifelong Commitment

My spiritual journey is a lifelong commitment to exploring and deepening my connection with God. It has become an integral part of my identity, influencing my thoughts, actions, and interactions with others. This journey has not only enriched my life but also provided me with a steadfast foundation of faith and inner peace.

Conclusion

The introduction to my spiritual journey marked a transformative period in my life. It strengthened my belief in God and led me to the profound practice of meditation. This journey has shaped my identity, guiding me towards a life of purpose, tranquility and spiritual fulfillment. As I continue on this path, I remain dedicated to deepening my spiritual practice and living a life aligned with divine principles.

❑

Chapter 3

The Winds of Change

The law and order situation in our village during the late 1930s was starkly different from what we experience today. One incident that vividly stands out in my memory occurred in 1938-39, when a young man killed his uncle over a land dispute. This tragic event shook our community to its core.

In those days, law enforcement was swift and uncompromising. The police arrived promptly, arrested the young man and subjected him to public punishment at the village gate. This method of dispensing justice was intended to serve as a powerful deterrent to others, making it clear that such heinous actions would not be tolerated. The punishment was carried out in full view of the villagers and drew the attention of onlookers from surrounding villages, underscoring the gravity of the crime.

Public punishments were a significant event in the village, as police presence was a rare occurrence. The visibility of justice being served played a crucial role in maintaining order and discipline. It was a time when the community's collective consciousness was shaped by such stark reminders of the consequences of breaking the law. The swiftness and public nature of the punishment were meant to reinforce the importance of law and order, ensuring that justice was not only done but seen to be done.

These events left a lasting impression on me, deeply influencing my understanding of justice and the importance of upholding the rule of law. They highlighted the crucial role that law enforcement played in maintaining peace and order in our community. It was a time when justice was direct and unequivocal, serving as a reminder to all of us of the boundaries that should not be crossed.

As the years went by, significant changes swept through our village and our lives. The independence struggle gained momentum and the winds of change were palpable. The zeal of nationalism and the desire for freedom permeated every corner of India, including our village.

Schooling and Patriotism

Patriotic Fervour in Schools during the Independence Struggle

During the struggle for independence, our schools transformed into vibrant centers of patriotic enthusiasm. As children, we were encouraged to actively participate in rallies, chant slogans and raise awareness about the freedom movement. These activities instilled in us a profound sense of pride and responsibility towards our country.

The experience of participating in these rallies was exhilarating. Chanting slogans such as "Vande Mataram" and "Inquilab Zindabad," we felt an intense connection to the cause of freedom. The stories of valiant freedom fighters, their sacrifices and their unwavering determination deeply resonated with us. These narratives were more than just tales; they were lessons in bravery that shaped our young minds.

As children, our understanding of the British Raj and the concept of freedom was evolving. We saw the British rule as an oppressive force that curtailed our nation's potential and stifled our identity. The idea of independence was thrilling and the prospect of a free India ignited our imaginations. We envisioned a country where justice, equality and opportunity were available to all, a stark contrast to the realities of colonial rule.

The sense of unity we experienced during those times was unparalleled. In our classrooms and playgrounds, discussions about the freedom struggle were common. We shared a collective dream of liberation and felt a deep sense of camaraderie with our peers. This unity was a powerful force, binding us together with a shared purpose and a common goal.

The Partition: A Turning Point

The partition of India in 1947 was a watershed moment in our history, marked by both the joyous news of independence and the horrors of communal violence and mass displacement. This tumultuous period left an indelible mark on our nation and profoundly impacted the lives of ordinary people, especially children.

As news of independence spread, it was overshadowed by the brutal reality of partition. The communal violence that erupted in various parts of the country created an atmosphere of chaos and dread.

Our village, like many others, was caught in the painful process of migration. Muslims who had lived among us for generations, sharing in our joys and sorrows, suddenly found themselves leaving for the safety of Malerkotla. This state, known for its historical legacy of protecting Muslims, became a refuge for those seeking safety amidst the chaos. The departure of our Muslim neighbours was heart-wrenching, as it signalled the tearing apart of a once cohesive community.

For children, the partition was particularly confusing and terrifying. The sense of unity and collective pride that had been fostered during the independence struggle was suddenly replaced by an atmosphere of fear and suspicion. The stories of heroism and sacrifice that had inspired us now seemed overshadowed by tales of violence and loss. We struggled to understand why friends and neighbours were being forced to leave and why communities were being torn apart.

The partition reshaped the social fabric of our village, altering the course of our community's history. It left scars that would take generations to heal. As children, we witnessed the devastating impact of communal violence first hand. We saw families torn apart, homes abandoned and lives disrupted. These experiences shaped our understanding of the world, making us acutely aware of the fragility of peace and the devastating consequences of hatred and division.

The impact on the common person was profound. The sense of security and stability that had characterised the village life was shattered. People who had lived side by side for centuries now found themselves on opposite sides of a hastily drawn border. The trauma of partition lingered long after the violence subsided, as families tried to rebuild their lives amidst the memories of loss and displacement.

Reflecting on those times, I realise how deeply the events of 1947 affected our collective psyche. The partition was not just a political division; it was a human tragedy that left an indelible mark on all who lived through it. For children, it was a harsh lesson in the realities of conflict and the importance of fostering understanding and compassion to prevent such horrors from ever occurring again.

During World War II, school children, including myself, were encouraged to persuade young men to join the armed forces. The slogans we shouted still echo in my mind:

"Yahan Milti Sukhi Rotiyan, Wahan Milenge Fruit, Ban Jao Recruit"

"Yahan Milti Tuti Jutiya, Wahan Milenge Boot, Ban Jao Recruit."

These slogans, translated as "Here you get dry bread, there you'll get fruits, become a recruit" and "Here you get broken sandals, there you'll get boots, become a recruit," were meant to highlight the better conditions and opportunities that awaited those who joined the armed forces. The independence struggle also saw us participating in rallies and slogans like "Inqalab Zindabad" (Long Live the Revolution), instilled a sense of patriotism and unity among us.

The war and the independence movement were defining moments in our history and being a part of these events was both exciting and educational. We learned about sacrifice, resilience and the power of collective action. These experiences reshaped our views and instilled in us a deep sense of patriotism, and responsibility towards our country and our fellow citizens.

Partition and Its Impact

The partition of India in 1947 brought about significant upheaval. Trains arrived from Pakistan filled with the bodies of Hindus and Sikhs, creating a climate of fear and tension. Muslims in our region began migrating to Malerkotla, a state known for its safety and respect for its Muslim residents. This tradition of protection was rooted in a historical act of sympathy shown by the Nawab of Malerkotla towards the sons of Guru Gobind Singh, ensuring the safety of Muslims in his state.

Malerkotla a Muslim Nawab state, was about 10 kms from my village. The target of Muslim population in India was to somehow reach the Nawab State. There was an understanding that Muslims who reach Nawab state of Malerkotla are safe. As per the incidence that happened at Sirhind when Shahzada's of Guru Gobind Singh were ordered to be killed by Britisher's, the Nawab of Malerkotla objected and said it is not fair to punish small children. What have the small children done? Because of this support the Nawab gained respect of Sikhs and Punjabis.

The partition was a period of immense turmoil and uncertainty. Families were torn apart, and communities were displaced. Our village, like many others, witnessed the exodus of Muslims seeking refuge in Malerkotla. This migration was marked by a mix of fear, hope and resilience as people left their homes in search of safety and stability.

Living through some of the most significant events in Indian history, I had the opportunity to witness moments that would define not just the nation but also my own life and values.

Despite these hardships, the dedication of our teachers shone through. Two senior teachers at our school, understanding the importance of uninterrupted education, took it upon themselves to organise free tuition classes at their residence in the evenings. Their commitment extended beyond teaching; they made arrangements for students to sleep at their homes, ensuring we had a safe place to stay and continue our studies despite the on-going turmoil.

These teachers became more than educators; they were beacons of hope. Their home became a sanctuary of learning, where we found not just academic guidance but also emotional support. The evenings spent there were filled with rigorous study sessions, but also moments of camaraderie and warmth. They fostered a sense of community among us, encouraging us to support one another during these tough times.

The sacrifices made by our teachers and their unwavering commitment to our education left a lasting impression on me. They showed us that even in the darkest times, the light of knowledge and the spirit of community could guide us through. This period of my life was not just about overcoming material shortages; it was about understanding the true meaning of resilience, solidarity and the power of education.

Their selfless acts of kindness and dedication have stayed with me, shaping my values and my approach to life's challenges. The war brought adversity, but it also revealed the strength of the human spirit and the profound impact of compassionate and committed individuals.

❑

Chapter 4

My Marriage

One day, when I was in class sixth, I came back from school my sisters told me I have been engaged. At that time, children were married at a very young. I was told I have been engaged with a girl from the neighbouring village. I didn't know the meaning of it at that time.

My would-be father-in-law gave one silver coin to my father and both agreed for the relationship. My father knew the family of the proposed girl. Those days marriage was limited to one's own community and people would not go out of community to find a match for their children.

Some of my school friends were from the village of my would-be wife. But I had never seen her village. Therefore, I was anxious to know about my future wife from my friends.

They used to tease me and used to take bribe from me to tell about her.

At this stage of my life, I often reflect on the profound contentment my wife embodied. She was a truly contented soul. I would frequently ask her if she wanted anything and her response was always the same: "I have all the clothes and jewellery I need." She never demanded anything from me. Her words, "I have everything," still echo in my mind. Though she left me in 2009, nearly 15 years ago, I feel her presence around me constantly, as if she continues to guide and converse with me.

My wife was a blessed soul, possessing all the humane qualities one could admire. She had an intuitive sense and often offered sound advice. Even during my challenging projects with the Government of India and the Planning Commission, I would discuss my dilemmas with her. She would listen attentively, encouraging me to follow my heart, avoid causing harm, and consider my decisions thoughtfully. Despite not being involved in my office work, her wisdom always shone through. By simply explaining the situation to her, I often found the answers to my toughest questions. It was remarkable how in articulating the complexities of my projects to her, I would discover the solutions.

I want to guide my young children with the lesson of compassion and support that my wife exemplified. She supported me wholeheartedly, managing all household responsibilities in my absence while I was studying. She never complained, always encouraging me to focus on my work and not deviate from my path. Her unwavering support and selflessness were the foundation of my success.

It's not the level of education or financial status that brings people together in a relationship. It's the commitment, love, faith, mutual respect and understanding that truly matter. In those days, completing the 10th grade was considered a significant achievement and someone with a 10th-grade education was seen as highly educated.

After our marriage, when we moved to Baroda, my wife began studying again. She travelled first time in life by train. It was a good inspiration from village life to a big city. She attended tuition classes with a local teacher and was dedicated to her studies and homework. I still have her certificate, a precious memento of that achievement. I could see the pride in her eyes, knowing she had done it for both of us.

At the family front, she never interfered how much money I spent on my siblings or my relatives. All the time, she was eager to help my sisters, brothers and their children. In whatever way she could, she used to help them when they came to stay with us when we were in Baroda.

My youngest sister Satya stayed with us in Baroda. she used to study here. She also learnt music at Baroda. I still remember one incident when both my sister and my wife were studying, and I didn't have money to pay tuition fees of both. Then my wife said, "It's okay, you pay for Satya. I can do it afterwards." She didn't make me realise that I was doing injustice for her. She happily agreed and it was all her efforts to get my sister degree as she was unmarried at that time and getting degree and education for her was important.

Those were the times when women used to sacrifice. Those were the times when woman used to think of a family as a whole; it is not the individual that has to be given preference, rather it is the family as a unit.

She believed in God and she used to do meditation and sit calm, and pray for the peace of the family. And in all the difficult situations, she was always with me. She was a perfect companion one can get. I was reluctant in the beginning but she proved to be a perfect wife and a perfect mother, an epitome of unconditional love.

A Night of Embarrassment and Love

After our wedding, Vidya was living with her parents while I focused on my studies. One evening, as I sat with my father at our shop, my friend Dharampal arrived with his wife. With a smile, he said, "Why don't you bring your wife here?" His words struck a chord with me, and I realised it was time for Vidya to join me. I had heard that on the first night together, a husband should give his wife a gift or some money. As a student with no income, I nervously took some money from my father's cash counter, thinking I'd give Vidya 5 or 10 rupees, or whatever she asked for.

That night, Vidya didn't ask for anything. We spent a beautiful evening together, filled with conversation and dreams for the future. I felt an overwhelming sense of love and connection with her. It was a perfect night, unmarred by material gifts.

The next morning, however, my father discovered the missing cash. His voice thundered through the house, "Hem! Hem! You have stolen money!" My heart sank as embarrassment washed over me. The entire family gathered, and I felt the weight of their eyes. My father was furious, not understanding the sentiment behind my actions. My mother was able to soothe and calm him soon by explaining the reason of my action.

Vidya stood quietly in the corner, her presence calm and understanding. She didn't need a gift or money to feel cherished; her mere presence in my life was a blessing. This incident soon became a family anecdote, often recounted with laughter, serving as a reminder of the innocence of young love.

My mother later confided in me that Vidya was considered a lucky charm for our family. Despite the embarrassing start, our bond only grew stronger. This experience taught me the true value of love, humility, and understanding in a relationship. Vidya's patience and grace made me realize that the most precious gift I could give her was my unwavering love and commitment.

Beautiful Journey with Vidya

Our marriage on July 2nd, 1950, marked the beginning of a beautiful journey. My beloved wife, Vidya, and I embarked on this path together, filled with dreams and aspirations. Our union was blessed with our first child, a daughter named Geeta, who was born in 1953 in the quaint village of Tandabada. Geeta's arrival brought immense joy and a sense of fulfillment to our lives.

Hem Raj Verma, Geeta, Vidya and Namita

As the years rolled on, our family grew. Namita, our second daughter, was born in Baroda. Each child brought a unique blend of love, laughter, and learning into our home. Anjana, our third daughter, was born in the bustling city of Bombay, and her vibrant energy mirrored the city's dynamic spirit. Alka, our fourth daughter, was born in Kanpur, adding another layer of happiness and harmony to our growing family.

After being blessed with four wonderful daughters, we welcomed our son, Somesh, into the world in Chandigarh. The joy of having a son after four daughters was profound, and perhaps, knowingly or unknowingly, I found myself pampering him more. Somesh held a special place in my heart, and I took great pride in his growth and achievements.

When Somesh reached the 7th grade, I saw an opportunity for him to broaden his horizons and experience the world beyond our immediate surroundings. I decided to send him on a cultural exchange program to South Korea for a month during summer vacations, a decision that would shape his perspectives and enrich his life in countless ways. This program exposed him to diverse cultures, ideas, and friendships that would last a lifetime. I am proud of my son.

I love my daughters. My daughter Alka left us early in 2014. She was a gem. I still remember her powerful words and remember how she used to take care of me.

Reflecting on these years, I realize how each child, each birth, and each milestone wove a rich tapestry of experiences that defined our family. Vidya and I cherished every moment, from the bustling streets of Bombay to the serene landscapes of Chandigarh. Our journey, filled with love, challenges, and growth, is a testament to the strength and unity of our family.

Life After Marriage: Our Struggles and Sentiments

After getting married, we shifted to Baroda, a city bustling with new opportunities and challenges. Life was simple yet filled with its unique struggles. Our home was modest, equipped with just the basics, including an 8-rupee stove. We had only two plates to cook and serve our meals, a daily reminder of our humble beginnings.

One of the most memorable moments in our early married life was when I bought Vidya her first saree. It was during a trip to Bombay, and I managed to purchase it for just 8 rupees. Despite its modest cost, Vidya treasured it that immensely. It was yellow with a black border, and she never demanded or expected it. She wore it on important days and ceremonies, cherishing it as a symbol of our love and the small joys we could afford.

Life in Baroda came with its own set of challenges. When Vidya fell ill, I took her to a nearby nursing home. We stayed there for three days, and the bill amounted to 70 rupees. To manage this unexpected expense, I had to sell her gold hair clip, but the relief of seeing Vidya discharged and on the road to recovery was worth every sacrifice.

Our early years of marriage were marked by these simple yet profound experiences. Despite the financial hardships, we found joy in each other's company and strength in our love. Every small victory, like buying that first saree or overcoming illness together, became a cherished memory, reminding us of our commitment to one another.

My father-in-law, in his immense generosity, gave ornaments of gold to my wife as part of her wedding gift. Our marriage festivities were grand, with the baraat staying at my wife's place for three days, despite the heavy rain. My father decided it was best to delay transporting the jewellery due to the bad weather.

When we finally returned to Manvi, our village, from Tandabada, we were happy to be back home. However, the story took an unexpected turn when my wife visited her parental home again. During her visit, my relatives decided to bring the jewellery, known as 'baree', back to Manvi.

But when they arrived, an alarming discovery was made—the entire collection of parental jewellery was nowhere to be found. My wife wasn't present when this happened, adding to the confusion and distress. The precious gifts from her family, meant to symbolize blessings and prosperity, were inexplicably missing.

This incident cast a shadow over our joy and left us grappling with a mix of emotions—disbelief, sadness, and a sense of loss. The absence of the jewellery, rich in sentimental and material value, was a poignant moment in our journey, reminding us of the unpredictability of life and the enduring importance of family bonds over material possessions.

My brother-in-law Jagan and I shared a deep and meaningful bond. We would spend countless hours talking, our conversations flowing seamlessly from one topic to another. Our connection was truly special, marked by a mutual respect and understanding.

Every summer, my children eagerly anticipated their vacations, knowing that we would all be heading to Jagan's home in Malerkotla. The town held a special place in our hearts, serving as a backdrop for many happy memories. The anticipation would build as the summer approached, and the joy of arriving in Malerkotla was always palpable. The children's laughter would fill the air as they played, explored, and experienced the simple pleasures of life.

We would all gather together, our extended family, and relish the opportunity to reconnect, unwind, and enjoy each other's company. The days were filled with activities, excursions, and shared meals, while the evenings were often spent in lively conversation and laughter. Jagan, with his warmth and charm, was always at the center of these gatherings, making everyone feel welcome and valued.

Those summers were more than just vacations; they were a time of bonding, relaxation, and creating lasting memories. The camaraderie, the shared experiences, and the joy of being together as a family made these trips truly unforgettable. The sense of belonging and togetherness we felt during those days remains a cherished part of our family history.

❑

Chapter 5

A Life of Learning

Early Education in Manvi

My educational journey began in 1936 when I first joined the Government Primary School in Manvi at the tender age of five. This modest school became the foundation of my academic pursuits and holds a special place in my heart. The memory of my first day is still vivid; my father held my hand tightly as we walked through the village streets to reach the school. I felt a mix of excitement and nervousness, but my father's presence and his unwavering belief in the importance of education reassured me.

From the start, my father was dedicated to ensuring I received a good education. His commitment was evident when he personally requested the Headmaster to admit me. His actions that day instilled in me the significance of learning and the opportunities it could bring.

The primary school was a simple building, but it was the hub of learning for many children in our village. I may add that this primary school was the only school in the surrounding eight villages. Children would walk daily to school in groups. The stress, unlike now days, was minimum during those days. At that time, the medium of instruction was Urdu. My teacher, whom we all fondly called Rabbi Master, was a devoted educator named Ravishankar. His passion for teaching and genuine care for his students had a profound impact on my early education. He nurtured my love for learning and encouraged me to strive for excellence.

Under Rabbi Master's guidance, I excelled in my studies. His dedication and effective teaching methods helped me pass the 4th class Board Examination with the highest marks in the Patiala State. This remarkable achievement earned me a scholarship from the state government, a significant honour that brought immense pride to my family.

This scholarship was more than just a financial reward; it was a validation of my hard work and a testament to the value of education that my father had instilled in me. It motivated me to continue my academic journey with determination and enthusiasm.

Looking back, the early years at the Government Primary School in Manvi laid a strong foundation for my future endeavours. The lessons learned, the values instilled and the encouragement received during those formative years have been integral to my lifelong pursuit of knowledge and personal growth.

Our journey to Patiala for the final examination was an adventure in itself. For many of us, it was the first time traveling to the state capital. Rabbi Master organised a trip to the cinema hall after our exams, where we watched a film named "Begum." This experience was entirely new to me and my classmates. The grandeur of the cinema, the moving images on the big screen and the collective excitement of watching a film together left an indelible mark on my young mind. It broadened my horizons and made me realise that education was not just about books and classrooms, but also about experiencing the world.

After passing primary school, I moved to the nearby village of Chaunda to continue my education from 5th to 8th class. This transition marked the beginning of a new chapter in my life. In the fifth class, I was introduced to new subjects, including Farsi (Persian) along with Urdu. This was also the first time we were taught English, a language that would become crucial in my later academic and professional life.

The middle school was about six kilometers from my village and we travelled to school on foot. Our daily journey was filled with adventure. During the winter months, the cold was biting and the water bodies we crossed were often covered with a thin layer of ice. Despite the chill, we found joy in our journey, often playing and laughing along the way.

In the summer, the return journey was particularly enjoyable. We would often jump into the rajwaha (canal) to cool off. Along the canal lived an old widow who offered us water from earthern pitchers and a fistful of boiled chana. Her simple gesture was always accompanied by a piece of wisdom: she advised us not to drink water on an empty stomach. This lesson in care and concern went beyond her humble offerings, leaving a lasting impression on us.

These journeys to and from school were more than just commutes; they were a time of bonding, exploration and learning. The adventures we had and the people we met along the way enriched our lives and provided us with cherished memories that we would carry with us forever.

High School at Khanna

After passing the 8th class Board Examination with distinction, I moved on to high school at Khanna in the Ludhiana District. From 1947 to 1949, I studied at this high school, which had a vast campus and provided hostel accommodation. The hostel life was a new experience, offering both independence and a sense of community. We engaged in various sports, particularly football, which became a favourite pastime in the evenings. The discipline and camaraderie of hostel life played a crucial role in shaping my character and preparing me for future challenges.

College Life in Moga

Upon passing my matriculation from Khanna, I joined D.M. College in Moga, located in the Ferozpur District of Punjab. My high marks in high school earned me a half-fee concession and a half-hostel fee concession from the college authorities, easing the financial burden on my family. At Moga,

I decided to pursue science, choosing physics, chemistry and mathematics as my main subjects. The rigorous curriculum and the stimulating academic environment at D.M. College nurtured my analytical skills and deepened my understanding of scientific principles.

Transition to Higher Education

At Moga, I completed my F.Sc. (Faculty of Science) and was promoted to B.Sc. This was a significant milestone in my educational journey, opening doors to higher education. I was selected for admission into the first-year Mechanical Engineering course. This transition from science to engineering marked the beginning of my journey into the world of technology and innovation.

Engineering at Delhi Polytechnic

In 1952, I joined Delhi Polytechnic, which at the time offered a National Diploma equivalent to a degree. The students, however, were keen on receiving a formal degree, and their collective agitation led to a significant change. The college authorities, decided to affiliate with Delhi University to confer degree instead of National Diploma.

The engineering course was challenging and rigorous, demanding both theoretical knowledge and practical skills. My previous education had prepared me well for these challenges and I thrived in the stimulating environment of Delhi Polytechnic, Kashmere Gate, Delhi. The faculty members were knowledgeable and supportive and the facilities were among the best in the country.

The Degree Struggle and Victory

During my time at Delhi Polytechnic, the agitation for a degree rather than a diploma gained momentum. The students argued that a degree held more value and recognition in the job market compared to a diploma. The Ministry of Education, under which the college operated, could not grant degrees directly. Therefore, the college had to be affiliated with Delhi University to meet this demand. The students' persistent efforts paid off, and we were granted degrees upon graduation. In 1958, I proudly graduated with a Bachelor of Engineering (Mechanical), a degree that opened numerous doors for my future career.

The Role of Teachers

The role of my teachers, especially Rabbi Master, was instrumental in my early education. At middle school in Chaunda, my guide was master Dwarka Dass, who was from my neighboring village Roorkee Kalan. Their dedication and passion for teaching inspired me to pursue excellence in my studies. The support and encouragement from my teachers at every stage of my education provided a strong foundation for my academic and professional success.

The Importance of Community and Family

My family's support was crucial in my educational journey. My father's belief in the importance of education and his efforts to provide the best opportunities for me were instrumental in my success. The community in Manvi also played a significant role, with the villagers encouraging and celebrating my achievements.

Lessons Learned

My educational journey taught me many valuable lessons. The importance of hard work, perseverance and resilience was reinforced at every step. The experiences and challenges I faced made me stronger and more determined to succeed. The knowledge and skills I gained through my education have been invaluable in my professional career and personal growth.

Moving Forward with Hope

With gratitude for the past and hope for the future, I continue my journey. The lessons of my early years in Manvi are the foundation upon which I build my life. They are a source of strength and inspiration as I move forward into the unknown. I am excited about the possibilities that lie ahead and committed to making a positive impact in my field and community.

The Story Continues

The story of my life is still unfolding. The early years in Manvi are just the beginning. As I continue my journey, I carry with me the lessons, values and experiences that have shaped me. The story of my life is a testament to the enduring power of a simple, honest and meaningful life. I am grateful for the opportunities I had and the people who supported me and I am committed to helping others in their own educational journeys. I learned a lot from Sh. Shaibhai Patni who as head of Industrial Engg. Dept. at Jyoti Ltd., Baroda, for which I truly feel blessed.

❑

Chapter 6

The Professional Milestones

The Crossroads of Opportunity

Upon graduating from the Delhi College of Engineering in 1958, I stood at a significant crossroads, faced with multiple career opportunities. My journey began with an offer from Diwania Industries, located in Kashmiri Gate, Delhi. The position came with a monthly salary of Rs.250 and the company was known for its compressor manufacturing facility in Okhla, Delhi. Around the same time, I received another offer from a company based in Bombay, which required me to work at the Koyna Dam in Maharashtra. Initially I had no knowledge of location of Koyna in Maharashtra. I thought it was a job in Bombay. They offered Rs.300 per month, but after some negotiations, they agreed to increase it to Rs. 350. This offer was particularly enticing due to the nature of the project and the slightly higher pay.

The Koyna Dam project was a joint venture between Indian and German partners. The German company, Salzgitter, provided technical support, while the Indian partners, Shah Construction Company and M/s Jolly from Bombay, managed the local manpower and construction materials. This collaboration aimed to construct one of the largest dams in Maharashtra, which would play a crucial role in hydroelectric power generation and irrigation.

Seeking Guidance

Faced with these opportunities, I sought advice from Dr. Moudgil, the Vice Principal of the Delhi College of Engineering. His guidance was invaluable. He asked me a critical question: how urgently did I need the money? I candidly replied that I did not have immediate financial pressures. Dr. Moudgil then advised me to prioritize learning and experience over immediate financial gains. He emphasized that working in the field, particularly on a project as significant as the Koyna Dam, would provide invaluable experience. He also imparted a piece of wisdom that stayed with me throughout my career: "Never build your edifice on the grave of others." This meant I should strive to succeed through my own efforts and integrity, without undermining others.

With this guidance, I decided to accept the offer from the company working on the Koyna Dam. This decision marked the beginning of a transformative chapter in my professional life.

The Journey to Koyna Dam

My journey to Koyna Dam began with a train ride from Delhi to Bombay, followed by another train to Pune. From Pune, I took an eight-hour bus ride through dense forests, with only small hutments indicating human habitation. This isolation foreshadowed the solitary nature of the assignment I was undertaking. Upon reaching Koyna, I reported to the Chief Engineer, Mr. Knob, a German national.

A Challenging Start

Upon my arrival, Mr. Knob expressed his reluctance to accept my joining report, citing an existing engineer who was being paid Rs.250 per month. He suggested that I accept a lower salary. Guided by Dr. Moudgil's advice, I stood firm and insisted on the agreed salary of Rs.350. I even asked for a written refusal if my terms were not met. Realizing the legal implications of retracting the offer, Mr. Knob hesitated. I proposed a solution: instead of lowering my salary, he could increase the other engineer's salary. Mr. Knob found this suggestion reasonable and promptly increased the other engineer, Mr. Shah's salary by Rs.50. Thus, my joining report was accepted.

Building Relationships

The next day, I met Mr. Shah and congratulated him on his salary increase. I shared the story behind it, which not only established a positive rapport but also laid the foundation for a cooperative relationship. Mr. Shah was pleased and agreed to assist me in all aspects of our work.

Learning the Ropes

My role at Koyna Dam involved working in a large stone crushing plant that produced aggregate for the dam's construction. I was assigned the night shift from 8 P.M. to 8 A.M., while Mr. Shah handled the morning shift. The initial days were challenging as I was new to the operations. However, under Mr. Shah's guidance, I quickly learned to handle belt conveyors, stone crushers and pump sets. The plant's machinery and the rhythm of the night shift soon became familiar companions.

Navigating Cultural Dynamics

One notable aspect of my experience was the workforce's composition. Skilled jobs involving heavy equipment were predominantly undertaken by people from Punjab, particularly Ahmedgarh and Ludhiana. This was advantageous for me, as most workers spoke in Marathi, a language I did not understand. However, the Punjabi workers spoke my native language, facilitating better communication and fostering a sense of camaraderie.

The Lessons of Koyna Dam

Over six months, I gained profound insights and practical knowledge at Koyna Dam. I mastered the intricate processes of the stone crushing plant and learned to manage a large workforce efficiently. The experience was enriching and laid a solid foundation for my future career. The dynamics of the work environment, coupled with my ability to adapt swiftly, prepared me for new opportunities.

Moving to Baroda

After six months at Koyna Dam, I received a letter that would change the course of my career. It was an interview invitation from Sayaji Iron and Steel Company in Baroda, Gujarat. They were keenly interested in my expertise in overseeing stone excavation and crushing operations. The offer was tantalizing, promising a monthly salary of Rs. 600, nearly double what I was earning at Koyna Dam. Moreover, the job came with free accommodation, electricity and even a servant, making it an exceptionally attractive proposition.

My adaptability and willingness to learn had positioned me as a valuable asset in the professional landscape. The experience at Koyna Dam had equipped me with the skills and confidence to take on new challenges.

A Twist of Fate

As fate would have it, during my stay in Baroda, I remembered applying for a position at Jyoti Limited, a company established in 1943 as an independently managed engineering division of Alembic Chemical Works Ltd. Curious about the status of my application; I decided to visit the company. There, I met the Personnel Manager, Mr. Mohan Bhai Shah. To my surprise, Mr. Shah informed me that interviews were scheduled in two days. He explained that my current salary far exceeded the salary offered for the position, which is why they had not sent me an interview call. Despite this, I expressed a strong interest in being interviewed, even if it meant accepting a pay cut.

The Pivotal Interview

Undeterred by conventional reasoning, I returned two days later for the interview. The day-long process at Jyoti Ltd. involved rigorous interactions with three company executives and engaging group discussions. I outperformed all other candidates and was selected for the job. After negotiating my salary, we settled on an initial increment, setting my starting salary at Rs. 275 per month. Faced with the choice between a lucrative Rs. 600 per month position with added perks and a Rs. 275 per month job without additional benefits. On deeper considerations for future whether to accept offer of Sayaji or Jyoti Ltd. And considering the future prospects, I accepted a lower salary at Jyoti Ltd. It was unconventional and challenging decision to choose the latter. This decision, though daunting at the time, proved to be serendipitous, unfolding into a transformative experience on the shop floor that would later serve as the cornerstone of my successful professional journey.

Arrival in Baroda

Jyoti Ltd. was known for manufacturing electric motors, pumps and water turbines. My role involved time and method studies for worker incentives aimed at increasing production efficiency. This position allowed me to delve deeper into industrial engineering practices and understand the intricacies of manufacturing processes. My work contributed to optimizing production and improving worker productivity, skills that would be crucial in my later career.

Joining Jyoti Limited

In April 1959, I embarked on my career with Jyoti Limited in Baroda, joining their Industrial Engineering Department. My responsibilities centred on conducting comprehensive time and motion studies, methods studies, and implementing incentive systems for various production staff. My primary focus was on machine shops, foundry shops, press shops and assembly units. Flourishing in this role, I garnered praise from my seniors for conducting detailed and impactful studies within the workshop. My innovative methods and time-saving strategies not only increased production efficiency but also led to higher incentive payments for workers.

The Pursuit of Higher Education

In 1962, three years into my tenure at Jyoti Ltd., the Government of India, in collaboration with the National Productivity Council, selected me for a study program in USA, focusing on Industrial Engineering and Production Planning. This opportunity was both an honour and a significant step forward in my professional journey. Generously sponsored by the American Government, the program covered the cost of my studies, while Jyoti Ltd. pledged to provide 50% of my salary to support my family during my overseas tenure. The US State Department in Washington, DC also covered my travel expenses. This opportunity marked a pivotal breakthrough in my career.

The American Experience

Studying in the USA was a transformative experience. I was exposed to advanced industrial engineering concepts and practices that were not yet prevalent in India. The educational environment was rigorous and competitive, pushing me to expand my knowledge and hone my skills. Beyond academics, living in the USA broadened my cultural horizons and provided a global perspective on engineering and technology.

The American education system emphasized on practical learning and research, allowing me to work on projects that had real-world applications. The exposure to cutting-edge technologies and methodologies enriched my understanding of industrial engineering. I made valuable connections with peers and professors, which enhanced my professional network and provided insights into global best practices.

DEPARTMENT OF STATE

Agency for International Development

CERTIFICATE OF ACHIEVEMENT

This certifies that, under the Program of the Agency for International Development of the Government of the United States of America in cooperation with other Governments,

H. R. VERMA

has successfully completed participation in a technical cooperation program

in the field of: INDUSTRIAL ENGINEERING

for the period: SEPTEMBER 1962 – MARCH 1963

ISSUED AT NEW DELHI

THIS 16th DAY OF SEPTEMBER 1963

ADMINISTRATOR

I delved into a comprehensive course in America, covering a myriad of subjects, including work studies, time and motion studies, job evaluation, production planning and incentive systems PERT-CPM, operations, research across various production shops and offices. Upon completing my studies, I returned to Jyoti Ltd., where I seamlessly integrated my newfound knowledge and skills into the company's operations. This period of professional growth and international exposure laid a robust foundation for my sustained success in the field of Industrial Engineering.

Returning to India

In 1963, after completing my postgraduate studies, I returned to India with a wealth of knowledge and experience. I was committed to sharing the benefits of my education with my country and contributing to its industrial growth. My time in the USA had equipped me with advanced skills and a deeper understanding of industrial engineering, which I was eager to apply in my work.

Back at Jyoti Ltd., I implemented the new methodologies and techniques I had learned in the USA. My contributions led to significant improvements in production efficiency and worker productivity. I also conducted training sessions for my colleagues, sharing my knowledge and helping them understand and implement the new practices.

Reflections on My Educational Journey

Looking back on my educational journey, I am filled with gratitude for the opportunities I had and the people who supported me along the way. From the humble beginnings in Manvi to the advanced studies in the USA, each step of my journey was a learning experience that shaped my career and character. I was chosen by the destiny and it was evident that I had earned this through rigorous hard work. There are no short cuts to real success.

The Role of Mentors

Mentors like Dr. Moudgil played a crucial role in my journey. Their guidance and support were instrumental in my success. They taught me the importance of ethical conduct, continuous learning and resilience. The lessons I learned from them have been my guiding principles throughout my career.

I also learned a lot from my HoD in Industrial Engineering Department at Jyoti Ltd. Mr. Shashi Bhai Patni who taught me lessons of Industrial Engineering.

Active Participation in Productivity Councils

Beyond the confines of my workplace, I actively participated in activities organised by the National Productivity Council and the Baroda Productivity Council. My dedication and expertise quickly earned me a promotion to the second position in the Department of Industrial Engineering of my company.

My contributions in these forums also garnered widespread recognition.

National Electrical Company Limited, Bombay

My journey in the professional domain continued with my appointment at Crescent Iron and Steel Corporation, a subsidiary of the renowned National Electrical Company Ltd, Bombay. Established in 1946, Crescent Iron and Steel Corporation had emerged as a key contributor to its parent organisation's success. Joining the company in the role of Assistant Works Manager, I was allotted a house in the upscale Khar area near Santacruz, Bombay. This exclusive locality, renowned for hosting the opulent bungalows of film stars, positioned my residence merely 1.5 km away from the famed Juhu Beach.

Life in Bombay

Living in proximity to Juhu Beach, a haven frequented by film stars with their sprawling bungalows, infused a subtle touch of glamour into my daily life. My family relished the vibrant atmosphere, indulging in the pleasures of one of the country's most renowned beaches. Within the precincts of Crescent Iron and Steel Corporation in Bombay, I assumed diverse responsibilities, overseeing production in various departments, including foundry, machine, assembly and marketing. Specialising in machine tools, grinders and electric hoists, the company operated under the guidance of a Works Manager, an Englishman with refined tastes. The Works Manager swiftly recognised my dependability and forged a strong rapport with me. Despite his sophisticated exterior, he revealed a sentimental side, mourning for days when his cherished pet dog succumbed to illness.

A Promotion and a New Role

After enjoying a comfortable tenure in Bombay for over two years, a significant shift occurred when I received a promotion to the post of Assistant Manager, accompanied by a relocation to the company's Delhi office at Connaught Place. This change necessitated a move from Bombay to Delhi. In my new role, I became involved in liaising with the Government of India and shouldering marketing responsibilities for the company's products in North India. Despite the prestigious nature of the position, I found myself yearning for the dynamic environment of machinery and production equipment—a stark contrast to the office-centric work in Delhi. Faced with this misalignment of my passion and professional responsibilities, I made the difficult decision to part ways with the company, marking the conclusion of this chapter in my professional journey.

The Impact of Mentorship

Mentorship played a crucial role in my journey. The advice and guidance I received from mentors like Dr. Moudgil and Mr. Mohan Bhai Shah were instrumental in my success. They taught me the importance of making principled decisions, staying true to my values and continuously seeking knowledge and growth. Their wisdom and support were invaluable as I navigated the complexities of my professional life.

The Joy of Engineering

The joy of engineering and working with machinery has been a constant source of motivation and fulfillment. The dynamic environment of production and the satisfaction of solving complex problems have been deeply rewarding. My time at Jyoti Limited, in particular, was a period of intense learning and innovation that reinforced my passion for engineering. The hands-on experience and the opportunity to implement new ideas and methods were instrumental in shaping my career.

The Power of Determination

Determination and perseverance have been key drivers of my success. Whether it was negotiating my salary at Koyna Dam, choosing a less lucrative position at Jyoti Limited for the sake of learning, or making difficult decisions in my career, determination helped me stay focused on my goals. The willingness to take risks and make unconventional choices often led to significant breakthroughs and opportunities.

Looking Ahead

As I look ahead, I am excited about the future possibilities. The experiences and lessons learned throughout my journey have prepared me for new challenges and opportunities. I am committed to continuing my pursuit of excellence, lifelong learning, and making a positive impact in my field and community. The journey so far has been filled with growth and accomplishments and I am eager to see where it takes me next.

❑

Chapter 7

Exploring Engineering Adventures

Discovering Indo-French Time Industries

During my tenure at the Jyoti Ltd., I found myself exploring new opportunities in the bustling city of Bombay. Among the vibrant landscape of the city, I stumbled upon Indo-French Time Industries, a unique venture that specialised in wristwatch manufacturing under the brand name Time Star. This collaboration with French partners piqued my interest, and I saw an opportunity to delve into a different industry. At that time HMT was the only company manufacturing wrist watches, which were very popular in the country. One of the directors, Sh. Shah, who was also involved in the Koyna

Dam project, recognised me and facilitated my entry into the company. Another prominent figure on the board was Sh. Hemraj Betai, a notable personality from Dwarka, Gujarat. His wife, Hiraben, was a dedicated follower of Netaji Subhash Chandra Bose and had played a significant role in the Indian National Army's (INA) struggle, even joining the Jhansi Ki Rani regiment under Captain Lakshmi.

The Watch-Making Industry

In this new role, I was entrusted with overseeing the intricate processes of crafting watch cases, focusing on dies and tools production. Although initially a temporary position, I approached my responsibilities with dedication, all the while exploring opportunities that would align better with my specialised skills in production. This period was marked by learning and adapting to the meticulous requirements of the watch-making industry.

An Enticing Offer from Hindustan Aeronautics Limited

My professional journey took a significant turn when I received an enticing job offer from Hindustan Aeronautics Limited (HAL) in Kanpur. HAL, a prestigious central government undertaking under the Ministry of Defence, was deeply involved in the production of the HS748 (AVRO) passenger aircraft in collaboration with M/s Hawker Sidley Aviation Ltd. from the United Kingdom. The AVRO aircraft was crucial for short-haul transport for the Indian Air Force. This opportunity presented a chance to engage with a larger, more expansive organisation, aligning perfectly with my expertise in production planning.

Joining Hindustan Aeronautics Limited

Upon joining HAL, I was appointed as the Superintendent (Planning) for Avro production, becoming the first civilian officer to hold this position. This new responsibility posed a formidable challenge, as I had to familiarise myself with aircraft intricacies, manufacturing techniques and the complex processes involved in aircraft production. The technical lexicon associated with aircraft components, such as the fuselage, wings, flaps, ailerons and rudder, etc. initially seemed daunting. However, I embraced the challenge with determination and a commitment to learning.

Navigating Organizational Dynamics

Managing communication within HAL presented its own set of challenges. The organisation was predominantly managed by Air Force officers with titles such as Squadron Leader, Wing Commander, and Group Captain and Air Vice Marshal. Establishing direct communication with junior officers without consulting their respective Heads of Departments (HOD) was complex due to the strict adherence to hierarchical structures. Consequently, I had to rely on the information provided by the HODs, lacking the autonomy to independently verify its accuracy. These initial hurdles tested my adaptability, gradually acquainting me with the nuances of the aviation industry.

Addressing Production Costs

Fate soon placed me at the centre of a significant issue when the Defence Ministry raised concerns about the escalating production costs of HAL-manufactured aircraft.

The compensation from the Ministry hinged on the actual production costs of the aircraft, augmented by a 10% margin. Ideally, the cost of each successive aircraft should decrease due to the learning curve inherent in the production process. However, an anomaly arose when the cost of the eighth aircraft exceeded that of the seventh.

Investigating the Cost Anomaly

Appointed as the Enquiry Officer by Air Vice Marshal (AVM) Amolak Singh Rikhy, the Head of HAL (Kanpur), I was tasked with investigating and compiling a report on the cost escalation. This responsibility was daunting, especially since I had only 15 days of experience at HAL and a limited understanding of its production processes. To address this challenge, I proposed recruiting fresh diploma holders to form a team that could efficiently gather information independently from the shop floor. AVM Rikhy approved my proposal, and within a week, I had selected and trained ten diploma holders from the Kanpur employment exchange.

Implementing Innovative Solutions

Applying techniques I had acquired during my time in the United States, I implemented statistical data collection methods with minimal interference from shop floor officers. In an astonishing three-month timeframe, I compiled a comprehensive report revealing that HAL had the capacity to manufacture three aircraft annually, a remarkable improvement from the existing pace of one aircraft every three years. This significant boost in production potential could be achieved without additional investments in machinery or manpower.

The Transformative Impact

This juncture marked a transformative period in my career at HAL. My findings addressed the Defence Ministry's concerns and positioned HAL on the cusp of transformative advancements in aircraft production efficiency. AVM Rikhy, impressed by my report, wasted no time in taking decisive action. He summoned all officers for a meeting and announced the implementation of my recommendations, showcasing confidence in my proposed solutions.

Restructuring the Manufacturing Schedule

My plan involved restructuring the manufacturing schedule to produce one aircraft in 52 months, a substantial improvement over the existing timeline of 156 months for a single aircraft. The ambitious target was achieved within a commendable three-year period. However, this success brought unexpected challenges, particularly a surge in demand for imported components that impacted the production schedule of the UK-based company, M/s Hawker Sidley Aviation. Concerned about the unforeseen consequences on their production schedule, a team from the UK promptly arrived to investigate the situation at HAL.

Recognition and Further Opportunities

The innovative aircraft production planning system I implemented at HAL drew attention from various quarters. A team from Bangalore also visited to study the new system, recognizing its potential for broader application. The method I pioneered, breaking down each product into smaller, manageable elements, significantly enhanced control over production and time management. This groundbreaking approach became a catalyst for change on the production floor, leading to its widespread adoption by various HAL units.

Embracing Change and Challenges

Embracing change and challenges has been a recurring theme in my journey. Each transition—from Indo-French Time Industries to HAL, and then to Punjab Agro Corporation—brought its own set of challenges and opportunities. Embracing these changes with an open mind and a positive attitude allowed me to grow and evolve. Each challenge was an opportunity to learn and adapt, and each success was a stepping stone to greater achievements.

The joy of engineering and working with machinery has been a constant source of motivation and fulfillment. The dynamic environment of production and the satisfaction of solving complex problems have been deeply rewarding. My time at HAL, in particular, was a period of intense learning and innovation that reinforced my passion for engineering. The hands-on experience and the opportunity to implement new ideas and methods were instrumental in shaping my career.

Reflecting on the Journey

The journey from Jyoti Ltd. to Indo-French Time Industries to Hindustan Aeronautics Limited has been a transformative experience. Each step of the way, I encountered opportunities for growth and learning, faced challenges that tested my resolve, and made decisions that defined my path. The support of mentors, the importance of resilience, and the commitment to ethical conduct have been guiding principles in my journey.

As I continue to embrace new challenges and opportunities, I am grateful for the experiences that have shaped me and excited for the future possibilities. The story of my career is a testament to the enduring power of learning, determination, and integrity and I am committed to continuing this journey with the same principles and passion.

❑

Chapter 8

A Transition in Leadership

As I reminisce about my professional journey, there emerges a distinct chapter that marks a pivotal transition in my career trajectory—a chapter brimming with challenges, triumphs and profound transformations. It was a juncture where I bid adieu to the familiar corridors of Hindustan Aeronautics Ltd. and embarked on an exhilarating odyssey into the dynamic landscape of Punjab Agro Industries Corporation. This transition wasn't merely a change in scenery; it represented a profound shift in my role, responsibilities, and impact—a metamorphosis that would shape the course of my leadership journey.

The year was 1969, and I found myself standing at the threshold of a new adventure, assuming the mantle of Chief

Projects Engineer at Punjab Agro Industries Corporation, nestled in the vibrant city of Chandigarh. It was a role laden with significance, thrusting me into the forefront of agricultural mechanisation—a domain brimming with untapped potential and formidable challenges. Punjab Agro Industries Corporation, a joint venture of Punjab State and Centre Government set up for promotion of Agriculture Production.

"My tenure at Punjab Agro Industries Corporation was more than just a job; it was a calling—a call to revolutionise the agricultural landscape of Punjab and beyond."

Leading projects aimed at enhancing the mechanisation of agriculture became not just a profession, but my raison d'être, an unwavering commitment to catalysing transformative change. With each project, I endeavoured to infuse innovation and efficiency into the fabric of agricultural practices, envisioning a future where technology would empower farmers and propel agricultural productivity to unprecedented heights.

In those formative days, the Indian agricultural machinery sector was undergoing a seismic transformation—a crucible of innovation and competition. Tractors, the stalwarts of modern farming, stood as emblematic symbols of progress and prosperity. Yet, they remained a scarce commodity, with only a handful of manufacturers vying for dominance in an increasingly crowded market.

"Amidst this backdrop, my focus remained steadfast on developing and implementing projects aimed at bolstering agriculture and empowering farmers."

Prominent players such as Escorts Ltd., Massey Ferguson Tractors and National Tractor were engaged in a relentless battle for supremacy, each striving to carve out its niche in the agricultural landscape. Additionally, the Indian government's sanctioning of tractor imports heralded a new era of possibilities, presenting farmers with a diverse array of options to fuel their agricultural endeavours.

Undeterred by the financial labyrinth, Punjab Agro Industries Corporation under my stewardship, embarked on a daring quest for innovation—an endeavour that would forever alter the trajectory of agricultural mechanisation in the region. Importing state-of-the-art harvest combines for the first time in the country from West Germany emerged as a testament to our unwavering commitment to pushing the boundaries of technological advancement.

Yet, amidst the allure of progress, we encountered a formidable barrier—the exorbitant price tags of these cutting-edge machines threatened to confine them to the realms of privilege, beyond the reach of the very farmer they were designed to empower.

In a bold stroke of ingenuity, we devised a revolutionary rental model that democratised access to these advanced machines, transcending economic barriers and empowering even the smallest landholders to harness the transformative power of technology. By offering farmers the opportunity to rent these marvels of modern engineering on an hourly basis, we unleashed a wave of innovation and progress that rippled across the agricultural landscape, forever altering the calculus of farming practices.

Yet, as we basked in the glow of our triumphs on the field, shadows loomed within the confines of the office—interdepartmental tensions, fueled by ego clashes and bureaucratic red tape, threatened to eclipse our vision of progress. Navigating the intricate web of relations between Central Government and State Government departments demanded not only technical acumen but also diplomatic finesse—a delicate dance that tested the bounds of my leadership prowess.

"Despite my best efforts, internal strife reached a boiling point, forcing me to confront a difficult decision."

Faced with mounting obstacles and a tempestuous work environment, I found myself standing at a crossroads, grappling with a decision that would reverberate across the annals of my professional journey. And in a moment of poignant clarity, I made the solemn choice to bid farewell to Punjab Agro Industries Corporation, knowing that my journey was far from over—that the path to transformative leadership was fraught with twists and turns, trials and triumphs.

As fate would have it, a new chapter beckoned from the neighbouring state of Haryana—a chapter brimming with promise, possibility and untold opportunities for growth and impact. The Haryana State Industrial Development Corporation extended a gracious invitation, inviting me to embark on a new odyssey as a Projects Officer—a role that would soon evolve into something far more profound, far more consequential.

"Embracing the prospect of positive change, I accepted the offer with an open heart and a steadfast resolve."

My tenure at Haryana State Industrial Development Corporation heralded a new era in my professional odyssey—a chapter characterised by innovation, leadership and an unwavering commitment to excellence. In the corridors of power, I found myself ascending the ranks, propelled by my unyielding dedication and invaluable skills, each promotion a testament to my steadfast commitment to service and my ability to effect real change.

From Projects Officer to Technical Adviser, and eventually to Managing Director at the State Mineral Development Corporation—a subsidiary of the Haryana State Industrial Development Corporation—each step in my ascent reaffirmed my belief in the transformative power of visionary leadership.

"As Managing Director, I confronted a fresh set of challenges, yet my resolve remained unshaken."

Leveraging my wealth of experience and strategic acumen, I steered the corporation towards its objectives with unwavering determination, navigating the tumultuous waters of industrial development with poise and purpose. My tenure was marked by a relentless pursuit of progress, a commitment to public service and a vision for a brighter and more prosperous future for the people of Haryana.

Looking back on that transformative period of my career, I am struck by the resilience and adaptability that defined my journey. Each transition—from Punjab to Haryana, from agriculture to industrial development—was a testament to my capacity for growth and reinvention. My diverse experiences, spanning different sectors and geographies, enriched my perspective and fortified my resolve to make a meaningful impact wherever I went.

"The challenges I faced, both internal and external, served as crucibles for personal and professional growth."

They tested my mettle, honed my skills, and instilled in me a deep-seated determination to overcome adversity. Through innovation, collaboration and a steadfast commitment to my principles, I emerged stronger, wiser and more resilient than ever before. In retrospect, my tenure at Haryana State Industrial Development Corporation was more than just a chapter in my autobiography; it was a defining moment in my journey—a crucible of transformation that shaped the leader I am today.

"And as I gaze towards the horizon, I am filled with a sense of purpose and possibility, knowing that the best is yet to come."

In the year 1975, I got a job offer from Planning Commission Govt. of India for the post of Director Industries. I was selected by UPSC for this job. I was promoted to the post of Joint Advisor (Industries), Planning Commission by UPSC in January 1981.

Planning Commission job was also very interesting, where I was a member of the licensing committee for Industries, member of the foreign collaboration Board, member of Project Approval Board, Capital Goods Committee, and many task forces set up by Govt. of India. Period from 1960 -1980 was very crucial for India . After coming out of problems related to partition, India had to prepare itself for development. Our relations with USA and Western Countries were not very cordial as these countries considered of India to be Pro-Russian. We had very difficult situation for Foreign Exchange which was necessary for import of technology and Machinery. Whatever foreign exchange India had, was to be judicially used for the purpose of import.

There were three agencies setup for development:

1. Licensing Committee
2. Import of Technology for New Projects.
3. Capital Goods Committee for Import of Machinery.

I was asked by Planning Commission to represent on these important Development Agencies to ensure that these Agencies adhere to our priorities for Development. It was very important for Govt. Of India to have faith in me to ensure our development process follows to meet our requirement and priorities.

I was also a member of various committees and task forces set up by Ministry of Industries etc. This job was very challenging and I got a chance of interaction with various senior officers in the Ministry of Industry, Finance Ministry, NRDC, CSIR, Small Scale Industries Development Corporation and Promotion Industries in States in accordance with our priorities & requirements.

I was also involved in discussions and decision making in various committees and task forces set up by Govt. of India for the purpose of assessment of funds for development of industries in various states and promotion of sick units to make them viable.

From planning commission, I was deputed to National Federation of Industrial Co-operation promoted by Ministry of Industry Govt. of India as its Managing Director. This corporation was set up by Ministry of Industry for promotion and development and marketing of products of Industrial Co-operatives. I worked in this corporation from January 1986 till March 1989 and retired from Planning Commission on superannuation in March 1989.

❑

Chapter 9

Foreign Visits

During my travels, I had the opportunity to stay with several families, each offering unique insights into their culture and way of life. These experiences were not only enriching but also provided a stark contrast to the practices I was familiar with in India.

Meeting the Lehmers

In November 1962, I had the pleasure of spending a weekend with Mrs. and Mr. Lehmer. The Lehmers were an extraordinary couple whose lives were deeply rooted in their values and lifestyle. Mr. Lehmer, of Scottish origin, played music in the church, while his wife, originally from Romania, was a talented painter. Despite having no children, their homewas filled with warmth and love.

They were pure vegetarians who grew their own vegetables and fruits organically, using their produce for their consumption. I was struck by their self-sufficiency and dedication to living in harmony with nature. Spending Saturday and Sunday with them, I enjoyed their delicious home-cooked meals and the peaceful ambiance of their home. Their hospitality and devout nature left a lasting impression on me.

A Memorable Christmas Celebration

Later that year, I had the privilege of celebrating Christmas with another family. They had two sons, aged 12 and 10, and their home was nestled near a picturesque, snow-covered hill. On Christmas Day, I joined the children for snow skating on the hill, a joyful and exhilarating experience. This celebration was filled with warmth, laughter, and a sense of togetherness that made it a truly memorable Christmas.

Weekend with a Generous Family

On another occasion, I was invited for a weekend dinner by a family who also included their friends in the gathering. Each family brought a dish to share, which eased the burden on the hosts and created a festive atmosphere. I had promised to bring a dish from India, so I took some Sabudana Badi with me.

When the dinner table was laid, I was asked about my contribution. I requested the lady of the house to heat some oil, and soon all the guest ladies gathered around the stove to watch the Sabudana Badi being fried. They were fascinated by the process and excited to try this exotic Indian delicacy.

The evening was filled with cultural exchange and culinary delight.

The family had three children: the eldest son was 11 years old, the younger son was 8, and their daughter was 5 years old. I stayed overnight with them, and the next morning, over breakfast, we discussed various aspects of daily life. I was curious about the children's pocket money and was told that each son received one dollar, which was equivalent to Rs. 4.65 at the time. I was also told that children also earn.

What surprised me was how these young children earned their money. The eldest son was responsible for removing snow from the footpath and driveway each morning, a task for which he was paid. Sometimes, he also helped neighbours with their snow removal and earned extra money. The younger son had the duty of taking out the garbage, and he too received payment for his efforts.

I learned that in American culture, it is common for children to have responsibilities and earn their own money from a young age. This practice cultivates the habit of working, teaches them value of money, and instils a sense of hardwork and responsibility. The eldest son also babysat his younger siblings when the parents were out, further adding to his earnings. The children saved their money to purchase items of their choice, such as musical instruments, bicycles, or watches, etc.

Cultural Differences and Appreciation

This approach was vastly different from the Indian way, where parents typically provide for all the needs of their children without expecting them to contribute financially or otherwise. The American practice of involving children in household duties and rewarding them for their work fostered a strong work ethic and an understanding of the dignity of labour.

I was deeply impressed by this method of inculcating the value of hard work and the importance of earning one's own money from a young age. It highlighted the cultural differences between the two countries and offered me valuable lessons that I appreciated and respected.

Overall, these experiences during my foreign visits enriched my understanding of different cultures and reinforced the universal values of hard work, responsibility and the importance of community and family support.

A Memorable Dinner

I was invited by a family to spend the weekend with them and they had also invited several other families for a dinner gathering. Each family brought a dish they had prepared, creating a diverse and festive spread. I had promised to contribute a dish as well, but instead of bringing a prepared item, I decided to add a special touch to one of their desserts.

When the dinner table was laid, and everyone began to share their dishes, I was asked about my contribution. I inquired, "Can you show me your sweet dish?" The hosts pointed to a custard-like dessert. Smiling, I took out a few silver leaves (chandi vark) from my pocket and carefully placed them on top of the sweet dish.

The addition of the silver leaves immediately caught everyone's attention. The ladies were particularly excited and curious. As they tasted the dessert adorned with the silver leaves, their excitement grew. One by one, they began talking among themselves, sharing their delight with friends.

"You know what I am eating? I am eating silver!" they exclaimed, with wide-eyed amazement and joy. The unique touch of the silver leaves not only enhanced the visual appeal of the dessert but also added an exotic flair that fascinated everyone.

Throughout the evening, the dessert with the silver leaves became the center of conversation. The other guests were intrigued and wanted to learn more about this special garnish. It was a pleasure to see their reactions and to share a bit of my cultural heritage with them.

This simple act of adding silver leaves to the dessert turned into a memorable experience for everyone. It highlighted the beauty of cultural exchange and the joy of sharing unique traditions with new friends. The warmth and excitement of that evening remain a cherished memory, illustrating how small gestures can create lasting impressions and bring people closer together.

A Disturbing Encounter and Its Aftermath

During my stay abroad, I encountered a troubling situation that left a lasting impression on me. One evening, I was invited to a home where a small child, just over two years old, lived. The husband worked the night shift and typically returned home around 4 a.m. On this particular night, I arrived at their home around that time and pressed the doorbell. The lady of the house opened the door and invited me in.

As I entered, I could hear the child crying in the adjoining room, which was dark. The lady directed me to the drawing room where another woman was sitting and watching TV. She introduced this woman as her sister, who was visiting. Curious and concerned, I asked about the child's distress.

"Don't worry about it," she said nonchalantly. "It's his time to sleep, and he needs to learn to stay in bed when he's told. We're trying to discipline him."

I was taken aback by her casual attitude towards the child's crying. Both women seemed more interested in their TV show than addressing the child's needs. Shocked and disturbed by their indifference, I left and returned to my room on the first floor.

The next day, while visiting the key club where I was a member, I noticed the same lady engaged in a discussion with another man. Her demeanour was casual, and the man she was talking to seemed equally at ease. This sight only added to my unease about the situation at her home.

A few weeks later, I encountered the lady again while on my way to class. Surprised to see her out and about in the morning at that time I asked, "Where are you headed? Shouldn't you be at home, especially when your husband returns from work?"

She replied with a surprising revelation, "I'm going to the police station to report that my husband has left me. I'm also claiming social security benefits. He usually comes home drunk in the morning, and today I've finally kicked him out."

Her words shocked me. The casual cruelty towards her child and now the revelation about her troubled marriage painted a disturbing picture. It became clear that beneath the surface of her seemingly normal life lay deep-seated issues. Her husband's alcoholism and her attempts to discipline her child harshly were symptoms of a much larger problem.

This experience was an eye-opener. It highlighted the stark differences in how people deal with personal and familial issues. It also underscored the importance of compassion and understanding, especially when it comes to the well-being of children. The memory of that crying child and the indifferent adults around him remains with me, a poignant reminder of the importance of empathy and the impact of our actions on the most vulnerable among us.

Memorable Dinner with Friends and a Cultural Exchange

During my time abroad, I had the pleasure of visiting a friend from my batch, Mr. Roy, who was a Divisional Engineer with West Railways from Bombay. He graciously invited several Indian participants from our group for a dinner at his place. Mr. Roy had gone to great lengths to prepare a delightful spread, including chicken and various other dishes. Additionally, he invited his landlady to join us for the meal.

As we gathered around the dinner table, the conversation flowed naturally in English. The landlady, upon hearing us speak, exclaimed with surprise, "Oh, you can speak American so well! I am surprised." Her reaction was a stark reminder of the common stereotypes and misconceptions many Americans held about India at that time.

At that time, many ordinary Americans had a limited and often misguided understanding of India. They perceived it as a poor and backward country, teeming with wild animals like lions, elephants, and snakes. These views were largely shaped by limited exposure to India's diverse and rich cultural heritage, often fueled by sensationalised media portrayals.

Our dinner gathering provided a unique opportunity to bridge this gap in understanding. We shared stories about our lives back in India, discussing not only the challenges but also the achievements and advancements in various fields. We talked about India's rich history, its contributions to science and technology, and the vibrant cultural tapestry that defines the nation.

The landlady, initially surprised by our fluency in English and our sophisticated conversation, soon became genuinely interested and engaged. She asked insightful questions about our country, eager to learn more about the real India beyond the stereotypes. It was a chance for us to showcase the reality of our homeland—its diversity, its progress, and its potential.

Mr. Roy's efforts in organising the dinner and inviting his landlady were commendable. It was more than just a meal; it was an exchange of cultures and an opportunity to break down misconceptions. By the end of the evening, it was clear that her understanding of India had broadened, and she had gained a newfound respect for our country and its people.

This experience underscored the importance of personal interactions in fostering cross-cultural understanding. It reminded me that while stereotypes can be pervasive, they can also be challenged and changed through meaningful dialogue and shared experiences. The dinner with Mr. Roy and our landlady was a small but significant step towards bridging cultural divides and promoting a more nuanced and accurate view of India.

I may add the important event that happened at that time was assassination of then President John Kennedy of America that shocked the whole world.

Encounter with Cultural Differences and Stereotypes

During my travels, I had the opportunity to stay with various families and observe their perspectives on global issues. One particular experience stands out, highlighting the cultural differences and prevalent stereotypes of the time.

The Magazine Sharing Initiative

One evening, I was invited to visit the home of a woman who ran an organisation called "Magazine Sharing." The woman was married to a qualified engineer who worked at one of the biggest steel plants in the world and was the head of a department. She took me to the basement, which doubled as her office. There, I saw about six tables, each cluttered with letters and old technical magazines. She explained that her organisation invited people from foreign countries for visits and exchanges. After completing their assignments, these visitors would return to their home countries and often write back, requesting technical magazines.

As the demand for these magazines grew, she couldn't keep up. She began asking her friends to donate old technical magazines. Eventually, the demand became so overwhelming that she had to go on radio and TV, appealing to the public to send in their used magazines. Her friends also pitched in to help. The letters on the tables were from people in countries like India, Pakistan, Afghanistan, Nepal, and Burma, requesting these magazines.

She proudly shared that she had personally visited many of the recipients in these countries. Later, she invited me to a party where she shared her experiences and showed slides and movies from her travels. The images depicted the harsh realities of life in various countries: children in tattered clothes playing in dirty streets, women in Pakistan sitting with their "atta" (flour) waiting to make "roti" (bread) on a "tandoor" (clay oven).

Conversations and Misconceptions

During the party, someone asked her what she thought was the biggest problem in India. She replied, "Cleanliness." Another guest turned to me and asked, "Mr. Verma, do you agree?" I respectfully disagreed, saying, "No, the primary issue in India is education. With education, most other problems will eventually be solved."

The discussion then turned to Nepal, which at the time was being influenced by some communists from China. For many Americans back then, communists were seen as invisible threats. Someone asked her if she had seen communists in Nepal. She replied affirmatively said, yes.

One guest asked, "How do they look?" The lady explained that they often wore long red shirts and had grown beards. The guest asked the lady, "How did you know they were communists?" she replied, "They were wandering aimlessly, and nobody was talking to them. You could easily tell they were communists."

This exchange highlighted the limited understanding and stereotypes that many average Americans held about India and communists and other Asian countries at that time. Their perceptions were often shaped by sensationalised media portrayals and a lack of first-hand experience. I may add the communists were a great deterrent to western world those days.

Reflections on Cultural Exchange

These interactions underscored the importance of personal exchanges and cultural understanding. The woman running the "Magazine Sharing" initiative had a genuine desire to help and learn about other cultures, but her experiences and the reactions of others revealed the depth of misconceptions.

Through these encounters, I realised the value of education and cultural exchange in bridging gaps and fostering a more nuanced understanding of different societies. While stereotypes can be pervasive, they can be challenged and changed through meaningful dialogue and shared experiences.

My travels and interactions with people from different backgrounds enriched my perspective and reinforced the importance of empathy, education, and cultural awareness in promoting global understanding and cooperation.

The Importance of Communication

In those days, communication problems were one of the biggest fundamental reasons for misunderstandings in families, social groups, official communication, and political organisations.

To convey its importance, Michigan State University organisation arranged a programme called "How Rumours Spread" to demonstrate the importance of communications in official and personal relations. There were about 30 participants from different countries. In this exercise, 25 participants were shown a five-minute script while five others waited outside. One by one, the five outsiders were brought in, and each had to relay the story they heard from the previous person. By the time the fifth person shared what they had heard, the story had changed drastically, illustrating the distortion of information through poor communication.

Encounters in America

While staying in New York at Times Square, I went for a walk in the evening and saw a man begging for money. In the U.S., beggars often hold their hats and ask for money. I wanted to take his photograph, but he refused. He told me, "Sir, you will take my photograph and show it in your country, and it will give a bad image of my country." His refusal showed a sense of national pride and patriotism despite his circumstances.

In downtown Pittsburgh, I saw a person selling a parrot with a rubber string, similar to what one might see in Chandni Chowk, Delhi. I wanted to take his photograph, but he also turned his back and refused. He said, "Sir, you will take my photo and show it in your country. It will give a bad name to my country."

Reflections

These experiences highlighted the importance of understanding and respecting cultural differences. They also underscored the value of effective communication and the pride individuals have for their countries, regardless of their personal limitations and circumstances. Through these encounters, I learned that while stereotypes and misconceptions can be pervasive, they can be challenged and changed through meaningful dialogue and shared experiences.

These stories are a testament to the rich tapestry of human experiences and the universal desire for respect and understanding. They have enriched my perspective and reinforced the importance of empathy, education, and cultural awareness in promoting global understanding and cooperation.

Cultural Exchanges and Insights

During my travels, I encountered various individuals and experiences that offered deep insights into cultural differences and the perceptions held by people around the world.

The Magazine Sharing Initiative

During one of my visits, I met a remarkable woman who ran an organisation called "Magazine Sharing." She invited me to her home and took me to the basement, which she had converted into an office space. There were about six tables, each covered with letters and old technical magazines. She explained that her organisation invited people from foreign countries for visits and exchanges. After these visitors returned to their home countries, they often wrote back, requesting technical magazines.

As the demand grew, she couldn't keep up with it alone. She started asking friends to donate their old technical magazines.

Eventually, she went on radio and TV to appeal to the public for more magazines. Her friends also helped by spreading the word. The letters on her tables were from countries like India, Pakistan, Afghanistan, Nepal, and Burma. She even visited some of these countries to understand their needs better and to see the impact of her work first-hand.

Later, she invited me to a party where she shared her experiences and invited her friends to hear about her travels. She showed slides and movies from her visits to various countries. The images included scenes from slums, with children in tattered clothes playing in dirty streets, and women in Pakistan sitting with "atta" (flour) waiting to make "roti" (bread) on a "tandoor" (clay oven).

Berkley Springs

BERKLEY SPRINGS, MICHIGAN – 1963

We were attending a program on communication organised by Michigan State University which was held in 5 Star Hotel where we were staying. The Hotel was on top of a hill. The town was about 5-6 km from the hotel. On weekend, we a group of 4 Indians decided to go to downtown to see Hot Sulphur Spring which was popular among the tourists. In the town there was only one taxi, which was driven by a lady, one had to take an appointment with her. We got appointment and she came to take us to Downtown. This was afternoon of December, it was very cold. We asked the lady to pick us up after 2 hours from near a particular coffee shop, in the mean time we went to see the place.

As it was very cold we quickly finished our walk within one hour instead estimated two hours by us. We decided to go to a coffee shop and spend some time while waiting for taxi driver. We ordered the coffee, the lady went to her supervisor and talked to him something and come back and refused to serve coffee, giving some absurd reason. We understood that this was because of racial discrimination as persons in our group had dark complexion. In any case our purpose was to spend one hour there, I asked if we could sit there for an hour, for which she gladly agreed.

In the meantime, taxi driver came and on our way to hotel I recited this story to her and she was very much upset. After dropping us in the hotel she went to the Mayor of the town and told the story to him. The Mayor came to our hotel and apologised and invited us to a coffee at his house. He also requested us not to report about this matter to our Indian embassy as that will give their town a bad name and we promised him that we would not do that.

Visit to Chicago

I was staying in a hotel in Chicago. It was -38°c when our group visited Chicago. The Michigan Lake was totally frozen and people were playing ice hockey on the lake. It was totally a new experience of me. It was freezing cold for us, we would hardly walk 10-15 meters and would enter a shop to warm up. We continued doing this till I reached our hotel.

CHICAGO – 1962

Chicago - 1962

Niagra Falls, Canada

Berkley Spring Michigan

On reaching my hotel, I entered cafeteria to take some coffee to warm up. Two young girls approached me and requested me to take subscription of a magazine they were selling. I promised to consider their proposal, provided they helped me find a hotel, as I was not happy with the YMCA hostel I was staying in. They happily agreed to help me, they took me in their car and visited about 5-6 hotels. At every hotel we went, we got a reply, "Sorry Sir, there is no room". I was touched by the efforts they put to help me find a decent hotel for me.

Journey back to India

On my way back to India, my colleagues at Jyoti Ltd., Baroda, asked me to break my journey in U.K. and to visit the Company Associate in town near London. I was received by the company representative. He took me to the town. Next day was Sunday and I went for a walk. A person approached me, he was from Hoshiarpur Punjab and he was talking to me in English. After sometime he took a letter which he had received from Govt. of U.K. and he asked me to tell him of the content. I was surprised when he was conversing in English but he could not read the contents of the letter. I realised he was not educated enough but he had picked up the language to converse in English. I asked him what work he is doing in U.K. he told me he is doing "Nakdoor" business. I asked him what that meant, I could not understand the meaning. He mentioned that he sells underwear, socks by going door to door, knocking on people's doors selling these products. I understood the meaning of "Nakdoor."

The after U.K., I visited Paris, France where I visited Eiffel Tower and other places. From Paris, I visited Frankfurt in West Germany. Some Indian friends in America had given some names of hotels which were economic and comfortable to stay in Germany. I saw two people with Indian like dark complexion. I approached them; one of them was from Pakistan and another one was from Cairo. On enquiring where they are planning to stay, coincidently all of us had the same hotel name mentioned in our diaries. As it was economical we decide to stay in one room. It was about 1 p.m. and thereafter we decided to go for lunch. We found that most restaurant were serving Pork. The man from Cairo told "Sir, I am feeling hungry, I am going to forget about my religion and eat whatever is available at the restaurant." I persuaded him to try more restaurants. We could not find any restaurant of choice till 3 pm, we ended up eating bread, butter and cookies for lunch.

From Frankfurt I went to Switzerland. Thereafter, I stopped at Cairo, Egypt and visited some pyramids, mummies and it was good knowledge for me. At the pyramids I enjoyed Camel riding. Cairo was not very impressive city. It was a very mediocre type. There I met a gentleman from Iran and he invited me to visit Tehran. Iran was ruled by a King at that time. His wife was considered to be the most beautiful women in the world. Tehran was a beautiful place, like any European city. I visited Tehran after 1973 again and it was total contrast with the original 1963 Tehran.

Visit to South Korea

During my tenure in Planning Commission, I had several opportunities to travel abroad for work, the prominent one was visit to South Korea in September 1985. The visit was part of an International Development Exchange Program organised by the Forum of Industrialisation and Rural Exchange at Korea Development Institute. I also had the chance to visit a steel plant, which was a key part of the Program. This visit provided valuable insight into the countries, industrial growth and development practices.

South Korea, Seol - 1985

South Korea visit to Steel Plant - 1985

Reflection and Legacy

Looking back, I realised that my story is not just my own but a reflection of the collective spirit of my village and the unwavering support of my loved ones. It was their faith in me that propelled me forward, even when the odds seemed insurmountable. As an advisor in the Planning Commission, I carried with me the lessons of empathy, community, and resilience that my village had imbibed in me.

My journey is a reminder that with dedication, hard work, and the right support, even the most modest beginnings can lead to extraordinary achievements. I hope my story inspires others from small villages and humble backgrounds to dream big and pursue their goals with unwavering determination.

عُقاب اے گھبرا نہ سے مُخالِف بادِ تُندی
لیے کے اُڑانے اُنچا تُجھے ہے چلتی تو یہ

baad e mukhalif se na ghabra aye uqab
yeh toh chalti ha tujhe uncha udane ke liye

"Fear not the strong wind that rises against you, O eagle—for it blows only to lift you higher into the sky."

This *sher* serves as a powerful source of motivation for those who face the hardships of life. In this couplet, the poet affirms that one should not be daunted by obstacles. Even within the word "*impossible*," lies the promise of "*possible*".

Life is inherently filled with challenges, and it is our duty to confront them with courage and determination. The verse inspires resilience, reminding us that adversity is not meant to defeat us, but to uplift and fortify our spirit.

❑

Chapter 10

A Life of Service

As I reflect on my journey through life, I am filled with a deep sense of gratitude for the opportunities I've had to serve my community and nurture my spiritual beliefs. My time with the Planning Commission allowed me to make a lasting impact on my beloved village, transforming it into a focal point of development and progress. This achievement, born from a lifelong desire to give back to my roots, stands as a testament to the power of determination and vision in creating positive change.

Yet, my contributions extend far beyond my professional life. The restoration of two ancient temples in our village became a labour of love, driven by my unwavering devotion to Kali Mata, the Goddess. What began as a personal mission to revive these sacred spaces blossomed into a community effort, breathing new life into our village's spiritual and social fabric. This experience not only deepened my connection to my faith but also reinforced my belief in the transformative power of collective action and shared purpose.

For My Village

One of my proudest achievements was making my village a focal point during my time in the Planning Commission. A focal point means a village that has been approved for a range of essential facilities and services aimed at the betterment of the village and its residents. This includes a high school, dispensary, post office, bank, grain market, fruit and vegetable mandi, petrol pump and religious places for community well-being.

I always felt a deep sense of responsibility and love for my birth place. From a young age, I harboured a strong desire to give back to my village and improve the lives of my fellow villagers. When I had the opportunity to be part of the Planning Commission, I saw it as my chance to make a real difference. I was informed by my brother and my childhood friend Dharam Pal that Manvi and neighboring village Lasoi were in active consideration for being considered for focal point.

On returning to Delhi, I wrote to then Chief Minister of Punjab and concerned officials, giving reasoning and rationale for considering Manvi over Lasoi. With great determination and a clear vision, I worked tirelessly to ensure my village received the necessary approvals and resources to become a focal point. This was not an easy task, but my unwavering commitment to my roots kept me going. I vividly remember the many evenings when the village sarpanch would visit my home to discuss the problems.

The Government of Punjab accepted the reasonings given by me and decided to declare Manvi as focal point in the region. As a result of this decision, my village has been bestowed with upgraded high school, Anajmandi, Government Dispensary with facilities of admission and treatment of patients, petrol pump etc. This single decision brought lots of prosperity to the region.

Two Temples: My Heart and Soul

In our village, nestled in the heart of tradition and history, stand two ancient temples that have withstood the test of time. These temples, once vibrant centers of spiritual life and community gatherings, had sadly fallen into a state of neglect. Weeds and shrubs had overtaken the grounds and the structures themselves seemed forlorn and forgotten. It pained me to see these sacred spaces in such despair, for I have always had a deep devotion to the Goddess.

Driven by this devotion and a desire to restore the temples to their former glory, I took it upon myself to lead a restoration effort. It was not just a project but a mission close to my heart. I began by clearing the overgrown bushes and shrubs, revealing the beautiful architecture that had been hidden for so long. The physical labor was intense, but with each weed pulled and each stone cleaned, I felt a sense of purpose and fulfillment.

The transformation did not stop at merely cleaning the grounds. I envisioned a place where villagers could come not only to worship but also to find peace. With this in mind, I created a park around the temples. I laid out lush green lawns, planted colorful flowers, and installed sturdy benches where people could sit and reflect. The addition of a boundary line not only provided security but also defined the sacred space, giving it a sense of sanctity and respect.

As the park took shape, it became more than just a restoration of physical space; it was a revival of our village's spirit. The once-neglected temples began to attract visitors once again. Families started bringing their children to play in the park, elders found a peaceful place to sit and reminisce, and devotees like myself had a renewed place of worship. The temples became a focal point of the community, a symbol of our collective effort and devotion.

For me, this journey was a testament to the power of faith and community. My devotion to Mata, guided me throughout this endeavour. Each step, from clearing the first bush to planting the last flower, was done with a prayer in my heart and a vision in my mind. The temples, now restored and surrounded by the beautiful park, stand as a beacon of our village's resilience and dedication.

In this project, I found a deeper connection to my roots and to the divine. It was a reminder that with devotion and determination, we can breathe new life into even the most neglected corners of our world. This experience has become a cherished chapter in my life, a story of transformation, devotion and the enduring power of community.

In the village where I grew up, two temples held a special place in the hearts of the villagers: the Shiv Mandir and the Kali Mandir. The Shiv Mandir, dedicated to Lord Shiva, is located just one kilometer from the Kali Mandir. From my earliest memories, I have had an unwavering devotion to Lord Shiva. This devotion has been a guiding force throughout my life.

As a child, I would visit the Shiv Mandir regularly. I felt a profound sense of peace and connection whenever I was in the presence of the Shivling. My daily routine included praying and cleaning the temple premises. I would carefully pour water over the Shivling as part of the traditional Abhishekam ritual, a gesture of my reverence and love. The courtyard, often littered with leaves and dust, was a space I cleaned diligently with a broom. Each sweep felt like a prayer in motion, a way to honor Lord Shiva with my actions.

Over the years, as life got busier, the condition of the Shiv Mandir began to deteriorate. The walls showed signs of neglect, the courtyard became overgrown, and the sacred space lost some of its former glory. Seeing this decline pained me deeply. My childhood memories of the temple were vivid, and I couldn't bear to see it in such a state.

Determined to restore the Shiv Mandir to its rightful condition, I embarked on a mission of repair and renovation.

This was not just a physical task but a labor of love. I mobilized resources and sought help from fellow villagers who shared my devotion. Together, we repaired the walls, painted the temple, and restored the Shivling to its pristine condition. The courtyard, once overrun with weeds, was transformed into a clean and welcoming space for worshippers.

The renovation of the Shiv Mandir was a community effort, but it also felt deeply personal to me. Each step of the process was imbued with my devotion to Lord Shiva. As the temple began to regain its former glory, I felt a profound sense of accomplishment and spiritual fulfillment. The Shiv Mandir, now restored, stands as a testament to our dedication and faith.

In addition to my efforts at the Shiv Mandir, I am also an active member of the Sanatan Dharma Mandir in Yojana Vihar. My involvement in this temple community has been a source of joy and purpose. Together with fellow devotees, we organize events, perform rituals, and maintain the temple premises. Being part of this community has strengthened my faith and given me a sense of belonging.

My journey with the Shiv Mandir and the Sanatan Dharma Mandir is a reflection of my lifelong devotion to Lord Shiva and the values of Sanatan Dharma. These experiences have taught me the importance of preserving our cultural and spiritual heritage. They have also shown me the power of community and collective effort in achieving meaningful change.

Restoring the Shiv Mandir was more than just a renovation project; it was a reaffirmation of my faith and a way to give back to the community that shaped me. It is a chapter in my life that I hold dear, a story of devotion, determination, and the enduring spirit of service.

Creating the HR Manvi Trust stands as one of the most rewarding and significant achievements of my life. Rooted in a deep-seated desire to serve and uplift those in need, the trust embodies my lifelong commitment to making a difference in the lives of others. The primary objectives of the HR Manvi Trust are focused on providing crucial support to underprivileged individuals and families, ensuring they have the opportunities and resources to lead better lives.

The Manvi Trust

One of the core missions of the HR Manvi Trust is to support the education of children from impoverished backgrounds. I firmly believe that education is the key to breaking the cycle of poverty and opening the doors to a brighter future. Through the trust, we offer scholarships, provide school supplies, and cover tuition fees, ensuring that these children have the chance to pursue their dreams. Watching them excel in their studies and gain confidence in their abilities is a source of immense joy and fulfilment for me.

Beyond education, the HR Manvi Trust is dedicated to improving the livelihoods of struggling families. We provide financial assistance, vocational training, and resources to help individuals gain stable employment and achieve economic self-sufficiency. By empowering people with the tools they need to succeed, we aim to foster a sense of dignity and independence within the community.

Another vital aspect of our work is arranging marriages for poor girls and specially abled individuals who lack the financial means to celebrate this important life event. We provide the necessary financial support, organise the wedding ceremonies, and ensure that these occasions are marked with joy and dignity. It is heartwarming to see the relief and happiness on the faces of these families as they celebrate their special day without the burden of financial stress.

My dedication to helping others goes beyond just financial support. I am always ready to offer my physical, mental, and emotional assistance to those in need. Whether it involves providing advice, lending a helping hand with physical labor, or simply being there to listen and offer comfort, I believe in being present and supportive in every possible way. This hands-on approach has allowed me to build deep connections with the people we serve, understanding their struggles and aspirations on a personal level.

The journey of establishing and managing the HR Manvi Trust has been deeply personal and transformative. It reflects my unwavering commitment to service and my belief in the power of community and compassion. Each initiative we undertake is driven by a genuine desire to uplift and support those who are most vulnerable. Seeing the positive impact of our efforts has been incredibly fulfilling and has reinforced my resolve to continue serving others.

Patron of Rajput Association

In addition to my work with the HR Manvi Trust, I am also honoured to serve as the patron of my Rajput caste association. This role allows me to connect with and support my caste brothers, fostering unity and solidarity within our community. As a guiding figure, I offer advice and direction, helping to preserve our cultural heritage and uphold our values. I am dedicated to addressing the specific needs of my caste people, providing assistance and support in various forms, from education and financial aid to organizing cultural events that reinforce our shared identity and pride. My deep-rooted knowledge of our traditions and values has enabled me to serve effectively in this capacity, ensuring that our community remains strong and cohesive.

Homeopathy: My Passion

For over fifty years, I have also been dedicated to the practice of homeopathy. I hold a degree in homeopathy and have used my expertise to serve the community, addressing serious medical issues with compassion and care. My journey in homeopathy began as a personal interest but quickly grew into a lifelong mission to provide effective and affordable healthcare to those in need. My patients have always been at the forefront of my efforts, and seeing them recover and thrive has been one of my greatest rewards.

President of RWA Yojana Vihar

Additionally, I serve as the President of the Yojana Vihar Cooperative Housing Society. In this capacity, I work tirelessly to ensure the well-being and harmony of our residents. My leadership in the society involves addressing various issues, from infrastructure to social welfare, and creating a nurturing environment where everyone can live with dignity and respect.

Friends

Friendship has also played a pivotal role in my life. My dear friend Ram Swaroop Verma, hailing from the village of Badla near Manvi, has been more than just a friend to me. We first met in a mechanical drawing class in the 10th grade, and from that very day, we maintained a close relationship for 75 years. Our bond grew stronger over the years as we traveled together with our families, forging a connection that evolved into a strong and mature relationship as one family.

With Gyan Singh and Bhabhi Surinder Kaur

Another significant friendship in my life has been with Gyan Singh, my room partner during our time at Delhi College of Engineering. He went abroad for many years and later returned to IDPL Hyderabad. We frequently met and shared a common love for literature, which became the foundation of our deep friendship. Gyan Singh was awarded the Sahitya Akademi Award for his book "Chand and Roti," a testament to his literary prowess and our shared passion for the written word.

With Ram Swaroop

I also cherish the friendships I formed with Samitter Singh, Nishikant Sharma and Vipin Jain during my college years. They have been my steadfast friends, sharing both the triumphs and challenges of life. Our camaraderie, built on mutual respect and shared experiences, has enriched my life in countless ways. We have supported each other through various phases of life, creating a bond that has stood the test of time. Each of these roles and experiences has profoundly shaped my life. They are not merely titles or responsibilities but manifestations of my lifelong commitment to service, compassion, and community. My autobiography is a testament to these efforts and the values that drive them. It is a story of devotion, service, and the relentless pursuit of a better world for those who need it most. Through every challenge and triumph, my guiding principle has always been to serve with love and compassion, making a meaningful impact on the lives of others.

My College Friends

Yoga in My Life

Yoga has been an integral part of my life, a passion ignited in 1953 when Dhirendra Brahmachari introduced the ancient practice to the public at ISBT Qudsia Bagh. This was a pivotal moment, not just for me, but for many who were seeking a path to holistic wellness.

Brahmachari, a revered yoga master, demonstrated a series of exercises that left a profound impact on my approach to health and well-being. Among the various techniques, two practices stood out: dhoti and jal neti. Dhoti, an internal cleansing process, and jal neti, a nasal irrigation technique, were revolutionary in their simplicity and effectiveness. These methods were designed to purify the body and mind, preparing us for deeper yoga practices.

Moreover, Brahmachari taught us four essential exercises aimed at detoxifying the body. These exercises were not merely physical routines; they were rituals that harmonized our bodily functions and rejuvenated our spirit. Each movement was deliberate, each breath mindful, emphasizing the connection between our physical state and mental clarity.

This introduction to yoga was more than just learning a set of exercises; it was a gateway to understanding a philosophy of life that promotes balance, peace, and self-awareness. It marked the beginning of my lifelong journey in yoga, a journey that continues to enrich my life with each passing day.

Through these teachings, I learned that yoga is not just a practice but a way of living that fosters a deep sense of inner harmony and connection with the universe. This early exposure to yoga has been a cornerstone of my personal development, influencing not only my physical health but also my approach to life's challenges and joys.

❑

Chapter 11

Reflections and Guidance

As I approach the twilight of my life, I find myself reflecting on the journey that has brought me from the humble village of Manvi to the corridors of power in Delhi. This autobiography has been my attempt to share the wisdom gleaned from a life lived with purpose, dedication, and an unwavering commitment to service. In these final pages, I wish to impart some advice to the younger generation, drawing from the experiences that have shaped my existence.

The Bedrock Of Family

First and foremost, I urge you to cherish and nurture your family bonds. My wife Vidya has been my rock, her unwavering support carrying me through the challenges of student life, international studies, and a demanding career. The love and stability provided by family are invaluable assets in navigating life's tumultuous waters. Cultivate these relationships with care and devotion, for they will provide you with strength and comfort in times of need.

Roots and Wings

Equally important is the connection to one's roots. Never forget where you came from. My village has always remained close to my heart, even as my work took me far from its dusty lanes. It was the desire to give back to my birthplace that drove many of my initiatives in the Planning Commission. Your origins shape your character and provide a foundation for growth. Embrace them, learn from them, and when the time comes, strive to improve the lives of those you come in contact.

The Power of Education

Education has been the cornerstone of my success. It opened doors I never knew existed and expanded my horizons beyond the boundaries of Manvi. To the youth of India, I say this: pursue knowledge relentlessly. It is the great equaliser, capable of elevating you from the humblest beginnings to positions of influence and responsibility. But remember, true education goes beyond textbooks and classrooms. It encompasses life experiences, cultural understanding, and the wisdom of elders.

Discipline: The Key to Success

In my years of service, I've learned the importance of discipline and hard work. Success is not handed to you on a silver platter;

it must be earned through perseverance and dedication. Wake up early, set goals, and work tirelessly towards them. The habit of discipline that I cultivated in my engineering days at DCE served me well throughout my career. It allowed me to balance my responsibilities as a student, a husband, father and later, as an advisor to the nation.

Health: A Precious Asset

Health, both physical and mental, is a treasure often overlooked in the pursuit of success. My lifelong practice of yoga, which began with the teachings of Dhirendra Brahmachari, has been instrumental in maintaining my well-being. I urge you to find a balance between work and self-care. Regular exercise, a nutritious diet, and practices like yoga and meditation can significantly enhance your quality of life and professional performance.

Duty to the Nation and Community

As citizens of this great nation, we all have a duty towards our country and community. My work in the Planning Commission was driven by a deep-seated desire to contribute to India's progress. Each one of you, regardless of your profession, has the power to make a positive impact. Be it through your work, volunteerism, or simply by being a responsible citizen, strive to leave your nation and community better than you found it.

Preserving Our Cultural Heritage

The restoration of the temples in my village taught me the value of preserving our cultural heritage. Our traditions and customs are the threads that weave the fabric of our society.

While embracing modernity and progress, do not lose sight of the rich cultural legacy you inherit. It is possible, and indeed necessary, to strike a balance between tradition and modernity.

The Gift of Friendship

Friendship has been a source of great joy and support throughout my life. The bonds I formed with Ramswaroop Verma, Gyan Singh, Nishikant Sharma, Samitter Singh and Vipin Jain have enriched my life immeasurably. Cultivate genuine friendships, for they will be your support system through life's ups and downs. These relationships offer perspectives different from your own, broadening your understanding of the world.

Leadership and Community Service

In my role as the patron of the Rajput Association and as President of the Resident Welfare Association of Yojana Vihar Cooperative Housing Society, I've learned the importance of community leadership. If you find yourself in a position to lead, do so with humility and a servant's heart. True leadership is about uplifting others and working for the collective good.

Lifelong Learning and Giving Back

My passion for homeopathy has taught me the value of continuous learning and giving back to society. Find a cause that resonates with you and dedicate time to it. The satisfaction derived from helping others is unparalleled. Embrace challenges as opportunities for growth. Celebrate your successes, learn from your failures, and always maintain a spirit of curiosity and wonder. The world is vast and full of possibilities - never stop exploring and learning.

The Importance of Adaptability

Adaptability has been a key factor in my professional success. The ability to adapt to new environments, embrace change and continuously learn has been crucial in navigating the challenges and opportunities I encountered. This adaptability has allowed me to thrive in diverse settings and remain resilient in the face of adversity.

Giving Back to the Community

One of the most fulfilling aspects of my journey has been the opportunity to give back to the community. Whether through mentoring young students, supporting educational initiatives, or contributing to community development projects, giving back has been a way to honour the support and opportunities I received. It is a way to ensure that future generations have access to quality education and the chance to realise their potential.

The Journey of Lifelong Learning

Lifelong learning is a journey that never ends. It is a commitment to continuously seek knowledge, grow and evolve. As I continue my journey, I am committed to lifelong learning and to sharing my knowledge and experiences with others. The pursuit of knowledge is a lifelong adventure and I am excited to see where it takes me next.

The Role of Guides/Mentors

I was extremely fortunate that at every step I was blessed with guides/mentors who played a crucial role in my journey. The advice and guidance I received from them were instrumental in my success. They taught me the importance of making principled decisions, staying true to my values, and continuously seeking knowledge and growth. Their wisdom and support were invaluable as I navigated the complexities of my professional life.

The Power of Resilience

Resilience is the ability to bounce back from adversity and continue moving forward. Throughout my journey, I faced many challenges, but my resilience and determination helped me overcome them. The lessons I learned and the experiences I gained have made me stronger and more determined to succeed. I am grateful for the challenges I faced, as they have shaped me into the person I am today.

The Importance of Values

Values are the guiding principles that shape our actions and decisions. The values I learned during my early years Manvi and reinforced throughout my career have been my guiding principles. They have influenced my decisions and shaped my character. I am grateful for the values I learned and the experiences I had and I am committed to continuing to live by these values and make a positive impact in my field and community.

Reflections on a Transformative Journey

Reflecting on my journey, I see a tapestry of experiences that have shaped my career and character. Each step of the way, I encountered challenges that tested my resolve and decisions that defined my path. The move from Koyna Dam to

Baroda, in particular, was a turning point that set the stage for a career filled with learning, growth and accomplishments.

The Importance of Ethical Conduct

Ethical conduct has been a guiding principle in my career. The advice from Dr. Moudgil to "never build your edifice on the grave of others" resonated deeply with me. It shaped my approach to my work and interactions with colleagues and clients. Upholding integrity and professionalism has been crucial in building trust and respect in my professional relationships and has been a foundation for my success.

Embracing Change and Challenges

Embracing change and challenges has been a recurring theme in my journey. Each transition—from Koyna Dam to Baroda, then to Bombay, and finally to Delhi—brought its own set of challenges and opportunities. Embracing these changes with an open mind and a positive attitude allowed me to grow and evolve. Each challenge was an opportunity to learn and adapt and each success was a stepping stone to greater achievements.

A Legacy of Learning and Growth

My journey is a testament to the power of learning, resilience and ethical conduct. The decisions I made, the challenges I faced, and the successes I achieved have shaped a career that I am proud of. I hope my story serves as an inspiration to others, encouraging them to pursue their passions, embrace challenges and uphold integrity in their professional journeys. The legacy of learning and growth continues and I am excited to contribute to the future of engineering and beyond.

The journey from Koyna Dam to Baroda, and then to Bombay and Delhi, has been a transformative experience. Each step of the way, I encountered opportunities for growth and learning, faced challenges that tested my resolve, and made decisions that defined my path. The support of mentors, the importance of resilience, and the commitment to ethical conduct have been guiding principles in my journey. As I continue to embrace new challenges and opportunities, I am grateful for the experiences that have shaped me and excited for the future possibilities. The story of my career is a testament to the enduring power of learning, determination, and integrity, and I am committed to continuing this journey with the same principles and passion.

A Call to the Youth of India

To the youth of India, I say: you are the architects of our nation's future. The journey ahead may be challenging, but it is also filled with immense possibilities. Draw strength from your roots, arm yourself with education, work with discipline, serve with dedication and lead with empathy. In doing so, you will not only enrich your own lives but also contribute to the progress of our beloved nation.

As I look back on my life's journey from Manvi to Delhi and beyond, I am filled with gratitude for the opportunities I've had and the people who have been part of my story. It is my sincere hope that the experiences and lessons shared in this autobiography will serve as a guiding light for future generations.

May you find the courage to dream big, the strength to persevere, and the wisdom to live a life of purpose and fulfilment. Remember, every great journey begins with a single step. Take that step with confidence, for within you lies the potential to shape not just your destiny, but the destiny of our nation.

As I pen these final words, I am reminded of a quote by Rabindranath Tagore that has always resonated with me: “I slept and dreamt that life was joy. I awoke and saw that life was service. I acted and behold, service was joy.” May you too find joy in service, purpose in your actions, and fulfilment in your journey through life.

Jai Hind!

❑

Few Words from the Family

Oh lord Krishna! You have bestowed upon us the austerity of a person who taught us to be strong and showered trust and empathy to become strong pillars to bear the load of every problem.

Babuji's life teaches us how to live and face challenges. Life is full of problems and hardships. When one problem ends, another begins and this cycle continues. To solve a problem, we need to find its source, which often starts in our own mind.

Sometimes we feel discouraged and our willpower, morals and spiritual strength weaken. In these moments, we need guidance from someone wise, like a Guru or family elder. Their life experience can help us navigate family and social relationships.

– Joginder Pal Jindal

I am the eldest daughter and I consider myself incredibly fortunate to be his daughter. My father is an extraordinary human being with remarkable intelligence. He has always been the pillar of our family, nurturing us into good human beings. Sensitive by nature, he skillfully hides his pain and sorrows, presenting a composed demeanor to the world. This strong facade is his way of ensuring that we, too, remain resilient in tough times.

I deeply admire his strong willpower and strive to emulate it. My father has a very pleasant persona, one that draws people in. His day would begin with a morning walk at 4 AM, and he would return home by 6AM. Later in life, he incorporated yoga into his routine, following the teachings of Dhirendra Brahmachari. He excelled in meditation, mastering control over his emotions and pain. No one could ever guess from his face how much he might be troubled inside.

His ability to maintain a calm exterior and his dedication to personal growth through yoga and meditation have been truly inspiring. He remains an enigma to many, his strength and serenity serving as a guiding light for us all.

– Namita

He is an inspiration who make us learn how to rise respectfully and gracefully.

– Dr. Sharwan Gupta

Daddyji, our beloved grandfather, has always been a guiding light in our lives. He constantly reminds us of the importance of taking care of our health and inspires us to be the best versions of ourselves every day. His stories about his hometown, Punjab, are filled with vivid memories and rich cultural heritage, and they never fail to captivate and educate us.

Visits to Daddyji's house were always a highlight for me, my brother, and our cousins. We eagerly looked forward to the delicious meals prepared by our grandmother, Badi Mummy, whose culinary skills were matched only by her impeccable sense of fashion. I fondly remember how she wouldn't step out unless her hair was perfectly coloured.

Daddyji's accomplishments, particularly his esteemed role in the Planning Commission, have always filled us with admiration and a desire to follow in his footsteps. His dedication, hard work, and integrity have left an indelible mark on all of us.

Now that I live in Ireland, I love to tease him that the ladies here would line up to be his girlfriend, given how handsome he is. This always brings a smile to his face and adds a touch of fun to our conversations.

– Preity

Daddy, you have always been my greatest inspiration and a pillar of strength for our family. Even now, you continue to inspire us immensely. I am yet to meet anyone as wise and open-minded as you. Despite being my grandfather, you connect with me so well that it feels like speaking to a very wise friend.

From supporting my first business venture to standing by my erratic decisions; even when those closest to me didn't believe in me, you were always there, offering unwavering support I never imagined I would receive.

Thank you for being in my life and for continuously inspiring me to strive for more and to better myself.

You are the most successful person I know, and I hope to achieve even a fraction of what you have accomplished in life and to live up to your expectations.

Thank you so much, Daddy. I love you. With love,

– Divyansh

Daddy's life story is a constant reminder that hard work and kindness truly pays off. His journey through life and his life's achievements motivate me to push my boundaries. His guidance and love make me want to be the best version of myself. Always caring and loving, he guides me with wisdom gained through his own remarkable journey.

He's super protective of the family and totally takes charge. Like, I remember that time when my brother Rubal and I prank called Daddy from a random number, pretending to be Dubai sheikhs saying we stashed gold in his car. Daddy didn't waste a second – he rushed to the driveway to move the car and drove it away, just in case these "sheikhs" showed up within the next hour to collect their supposed gold!

– Gagan

In reflecting upon the life and legacy of our beloved father and grandfather, Daddy, we are filled with immense pride and admiration. Daddy's distinguished career and educational achievements are a testament to his remarkable dedication and intellect. Despite his advanced age of 93, he remains a beacon of vitality and sharpness, exemplifying a commitment to health that extends beyond mere longevity. His passion for homeopathy, pursued with the same zeal and focus that characterized his professional life, reflects a deep-seated dedication to holistic well-being.

Originating from the humble village of Manvi, Daddy's journey to the vibrant city of Delhi is nothing short of inspirational. Today, we are residing in the hustle and bustle of Delhi because of his hardwork and diligence. His resilience and determination enabled him to provide a nurturing environment for us, ensuring that we had every opportunity to flourish. His unwavering support and profound wisdom have been cornerstones of our family's success and happiness.

We, his family - his children and grandchildren are profoundly grateful for the strength, love, and guidance Daddy has bestowed upon us. His life story serves as a powerful reminder of what one can achieve with passion, perseverance, and an enduring commitment to one's values and to self.

– Somesh, Simi, Ishita and Dhruv Verma

❑